Marry
Me at
Christmas

Also by Susan Mallery

Fool's Gold

Thrill Me
Kiss Me
Hold Me
Until We Touch
Before We Kiss
When We Met
Christmas on 4th Street
Three Little Words
Two of a Kind
Just One Kiss
A Fool's Gold Christmas
All Summer Long
Summer Nights
Summer Days
Only His
Only Yours
Only Mine
Finding Perfect
Almost Perfect
Chasing Perfect

Blackberry Island

Evening Stars
Three Sisters
Barefoot Season

Mischief Bay

The Girls of Mischief Bay

To see the complete list of titles available from Susan Mallery, please visit SusanMallery.com.

SUSAN MALLERY

Marry Me at Christmas

HQN™

ISBN-13: 978-0-373-78850-7

Marry Me at Christmas

www.HQNBooks.com

Printed in U.S.A.

I'm one of the luckiest authors in the world.
Seriously, I have the best readers anywhere.
This book is dedicated to the delightful, creative and fun
Kim V.R. I'm thrilled that your girls week friends,
radiation friends and Inez got you addicted to romance,
and I adored meeting you.

And...

To reader Paula B, who asked that this book be
"dedicated to my son Tom B for making my dream come true."

❧ ONE ❧

"Do they know they look like pumpkins?"

Madeline Krug appreciated that Rosalind asked the question very softly. One of the first rules of running a successful wedding gown store was to not insult the bride or her wedding party. And while she normally would have mentioned that to her assistant, in this case the question was kind of legitimate.

It wasn't just the very full skirt on the bridesmaids' dresses. A billowing that was oddly, well, pumpkin shaped. It wasn't the colors, which ranged from tangerine to coral to, um, pumpkin. But when those two elements were put together with a pale green crown of leaves and tiny flowers on each of their six heads, the overall effect was just a little...pumpkiny.

"The bride told me this is exactly what she wanted," Madeline murmured. "That she's been dreaming about her wedding since she was a little girl and these are the dresses she pictured. She was thrilled we could find them."

Madeline smiled at her assistant. "Every bride has a perfect dress and a vision for what she wants her wedding party to look like. Our job is to find out what that dream is and make it come true."

Rosalind looked doubtful, but nodded, as if taking mental notes.

The fortysomething brunette had been working at Paper Moon for about a month now. With her kids all in middle and high school, she'd wanted to return to the workforce. Madeline needed someone she could depend on and Rosalind came with good references. So far, they were doing well as a team, although Rosalind still found the various bridal idiosyncrasies surprising.

Madeline returned her attention to the wedding party. She double-checked the fit of each dress, confirmed the bride was giddy with happiness, then promised a final pressing before the dresses were picked up the Wednesday before Thanksgiving. Because the, um, pumpkin wedding was the Saturday after the holiday.

By three o'clock the bridal party had left. Madeline retreated to her office to finish up some paperwork. After processing invoices, confirming a couple of deliveries and noting when her favorite bridal designer's new summer collection would be available, she leaned back in her chair and allowed herself a rare moment of contentment.

She loved her job. She wasn't saving the world or finding a new source of renewable energy—but in her own small way, she helped people be happy. Brides came in all shapes, sizes and temperaments, but for the most part, she loved each one of them. She loved the look on their faces when they found the right dress. The happy tears were so satisfying.

Sure there was drama, but she could handle a little drama. It kept things interesting. And when the drama was over and the bride emailed her a picture of herself on the big day, well, nothing was sweeter.

She was just plain lucky, she thought. If not in love, then certainly in every other part of her life. Because—

"Hello, Madeline."

Two simple words spoken in a kind voice. That should have been fine. Or even nice. Instead, Madeline stared at the well-dressed woman standing in the doorway of her office and knew that her life was about to change. She couldn't say how or why, but as surely as the sun would rise in the east, when Mayor Marsha Tilson showed up looking slightly expectant, things happened.

"Ma'am," Madeline said, instantly coming to her feet.

Because that was how she'd been raised. You stood when an older person came in the room.

Mayor Marsha had been the mayor of Fool's Gold for longer than Madeline had been alive. She was, in fact, California's longest serving mayor. She was much loved, warm, caring and had a way of knowing things that no one had ever been able to explain. Madeline had always liked her. She found her a little scary, but she liked her.

"Do you have a minute?" the mayor asked, already walking into the small office and taking a seat.

"Of course."

Madeline was a little relieved when Dellina Ridge, Fool's Gold's event planner, followed the mayor into her office and offered a reassuring smile. Dellina was a good friend. If something bad was about to happen, not only would Dellina have warned her but she would have offered moral support and brownies.

"As you know," Mayor Marsha began when they were all seated, "the holidays are a busy time here in town."

Madeline nodded. Fool's Gold loved to celebrate in every way possible. From mid-November until after the first of the year, there was always something going on. Lucky for her, it was an especially slow time at Paper Moon, which meant she got to enjoy everything going on around her.

The rhythm of a bridal shop was different from regular retail. Come January second, when a lot of stores slowed down, she would be juggling newly engaged brides-to-be. Many a proposal would be made on either Christmas Eve or New Year's Eve. But that wasn't why the mayor was here.

Mayor Marsha glanced at Dellina, who scooted to the front of her chair and gave another smile.

"It's me," Dellina admitted, sounding a little rueful. "I'm totally scrambling. The Hendrix family is planning a huge party on New Year's Eve, there are a dozen holiday events and three weddings, and I'm up to my eyebrows in invitations and details. I can't take on one more thing."

Madeline still wasn't sure where this was all going. "If you need me to help with something, I'm happy to," she said slowly. Of course she would be there for her friend. But why wouldn't Dellina have come to her directly? They'd known each other all their lives. Why involve the mayor?

Dellina shifted slightly. "Yes, well, it's more than my usual panicked call to come stuff goodie bags. It's a wedding."

Madeline looked between the two of them. "I don't understand," she admitted.

"There's going to be a wedding the Saturday after

Christmas," the mayor said happily. "You know how I love a wedding. This will be a small affair. Right now the guest list is at forty. I suspect it will grow a little, but shouldn't be more than fifty or fifty-five people. There's no location issue—everything will be at the bride's brother's house. The catering is taken care of."

"Ana Raquel is handling that," Dellina added. "She had a cancellation and can fit in the wedding. So it's just the basic details. Dress, invitations, decorations. I know it's a lot to ask…" Her friend shook her head. "I'm sorry. We haven't asked yet, have we?"

Mayor Marsha patted Dellina's hand. "I'll do the asking, dear. Madeline, your town needs you to plan a wedding. Are you up for it?"

"I don't know," Madeline admitted. "I've never done anything like that before. I work with brides and we talk details, but to take a wedding from start to finish, even a small one, would be challenging."

Which was as close to saying no as she was going to get, she thought as the mayor continued to look at her with that steady, supportive *You'll do what I say because I have powers and you've never once refused me anything* look that was both famous and inescapable.

"I have a master list and I'd be happy to help," Dellina added. "I'm sorry to put you in this position."

"Don't apologize," Mayor Marsha said firmly. "I'm to blame. When I spoke with Dellina earlier today and she said she wasn't available, we brainstormed who we could ask. You're the one we both thought of."

Madeline got the subtext of the message. Dellina had been as trapped as she was now. When Mayor Marsha wanted something done, she was unstoppable. Which meant saying no wasn't an option.

Planning a wedding in seven weeks, over the holidays, when she'd never done much more than be a bridesmaid and sell wedding dresses? Were they crazy?

"Sure," she said easily. "I'm in." She frowned as she realized she didn't know anyone who had recently gotten engaged, or even who was planning a holiday wedding. "Oh, who's getting married?"

"Ginger Blaze."

The name meant nothing. "She's not local. Is her fiancé…"

Madeline felt her heart stop. Physically stop. There had been steady beating, then nothing. That was followed by a distinct popping sound in her ears along with panic. Cold, slimy, I-can't-breathe panic.

"Blaze," she whispered. Quite the trick what with her heart stopped and her lungs not working. "Blaze as in *Jonny* Blaze?"

Mayor Marsha nodded. "Ginger is his younger sister. I believe she lives in San Francisco. She's in a PhD program. Something with biology or genetics. Mr. Blaze wasn't clear. However, he asked me to help him find someone to plan the wedding with him. That's when I approached Dellina. You know the rest, my dear."

Jonny Blaze? The tall, handsome action-movie star who had recently moved to a ranch outside of town? The man who had a body like a god and a smile that reduced perfectly intelligent, articulate women to puddles? Jonny Blaze, who was, unbeknownst to him, of course, her movie-star boyfriend?

No. She couldn't. She had a mad crush on him. Every time she'd seen him in town, she'd stared like an idiot. She'd babbled and he hadn't been closer than twenty-five feet. She couldn't imagine being next to him, let alone working with him.

I can't. There. She'd said it. Or at least thought it. Which was practically the same thing. She couldn't.

"From what I can tell, Mr. Blaze is a very nice man," the mayor was saying. "He wants to fit in. Be a part of the community. As you know, we take the well-being of our citizens very seriously. Mr. Blaze needs a refuge from the trappings of his career and we can provide that. The quiet, everyday kind of life he craves."

"The wedding is going to be close friends and family," Dellina added. "It's small and intimate. I swear, if I had an extra second, I'd take it on."

"You're already doing too much," Madeline said, pleased she could speak. "I know you. You're running in forty-five directions."

If it were anyone else, she thought frantically. But it wasn't and saying no had never been an option.

She drew in a breath and told herself she was strong. She was mature. At the very least, she could keep from squealing in his presence.

"I'm happy to help," she said.

"Excellent." Mayor Marsha nodded. "You're meeting with him in an hour."

Of course she was, Madeline thought, not even surprised. Because that was how the mayor got things done. A well-planned ambush followed by a lack of time to come to one's senses.

An hour. Not nearly enough time to lose five pounds, have a makeover and become glamorous and sophisticated. Why, oh, why hadn't she learned French? Or aikido? Anything that would make her interesting for Jonny Blaze? She briefly wondered if aikido was the martial arts training or the dog breed, then sighed. Too late to worry about that now. As it was, she was going to be stuck being herself.

"I'm going to tell him I don't have any experience with planning a wedding," she said. "I need to be honest about that."

The mayor smiled. "I would expect no less, my dear."

Jonny Blaze had traveled all over the world. He was used to the insular world of a movie set and the contrast of whatever town they were in during filming. He'd lived in tents, high-rises and, for six gut-churning weeks, on a fishing boat. But none of that had prepared him for the quirky, busy, oddly happy place that was Fool's Gold.

Everyone here was…nice. They said hello to each other, knew each other's kids' names and, as far as he could tell, celebrated every known holiday and a few he'd never heard of. He'd been looking for a place to hide and instead he'd found himself in an unusual town that he couldn't seem to ignore, but also couldn't bring himself to embrace. It was an unexpected conundrum.

He stepped into Brew-haha for his two o'clock meeting. The barista greeted him by name and asked if he wanted his usual. Had he been anywhere else, he would have known she'd remembered his usual because of his movie-star status. Except in Fool's Gold, the barista treated everyone exactly the same. An experience so re-freshing that coming to the local coffee shop became one of his favorite things to do when he was in town.

He paid for his order, then went to wait. Because this wasn't LA where a starstruck employee raced to get him his coffee. He had a turn, just like everyone else.

Jonny had grown up normal, so he'd been unprepared for how starring in action movies would change every-thing about his life. Now, over a decade later, he was used to slipping into restaurants through a back door and knowing paparazzi were going to be lurking around every corner. He'd tried living in a secure condo, then had bought the obligatory walled estate, high in the Hol-lywood Hills. When that didn't keep out the unwelcome, he'd gone looking for something better.

He'd found it about twenty-five miles outside of Fool's Gold, California, on a cattle ranch with a rambling old house and a barn that he'd converted to a shop and work-out room. He was close enough to town that he could get his normal fix at Brew-haha, but far enough away that he could revel in the quiet.

He'd sold the cattle to another rancher and had leased the grazing rights to the same guy. Now, as Jonny took his coffee, he grinned. Yup, he had grazing rights. What could be more middle America than that?

He turned his attention to the half-dozen tables at the small coffee shop. He was supposed to be meeting a Madeline Krug. The mayor had recommended her to help him plan his sister's wedding.

He didn't see anyone fitting her description, so he claimed one of the two empty tables. He figured she would find him when she arrived.

The store had big windows and shelves on the walls. There were a few items for sale, along with some harvest decorations. He saw pumpkins and a couple of ceramic turkeys. On one of the windowsills was a small replica of the *Bluenose*, a famous racing and fishing schooner from Nova Scotia.

As he sipped his latte, he tried to recall how, exactly, the mayor had found out about his sister. He didn't remember mentioning Ginger or her engagement, but he must have because it wasn't public knowledge. Maybe his friend Shep had said something. All he knew for sure was one minute he and the mayor had been talking about the upcoming Thanksgiving parade and the next she'd been asking about Ginger's wedding. He'd admitted he was lost when it came to planning, and before he'd known it, the mayor had offered to find someone who could help. Not two hours later, she'd set up this meeting.

The door to Brew-haha opened and a woman entered.

She was in her late twenties, with shoulder-length blond hair and blue eyes. She looked slightly rushed and a little frazzled. Not nervous, he thought as he studied her. More determined, with a little unsure thrown in.

Her gaze landed on him. Instantly her shoulders squared and her chin went up. Madeline, he thought, recognizing her from the mayor's description and appreciating how she looked more resigned than thrilled. He supposed most people wanted to be liked. He did, too, but for the right reasons. Anyone who was impressed the second they met him left him looking for the closest exit. Because they weren't there for him. They were there for Jonny Blaze, Action Star. Wariness was a lot more honest than gushing, and in his world, honesty was a sought-after commodity.

Madeline crossed the small café and stopped by his table. Her gaze was direct as she offered him a slight smile. "Mr. Blaze, I'm Madeline Krug. Mayor Marsha said you'd be expecting me."

"Jonny," he said easily, rising and pulling out a chair for her. "Nice to meet you."

"Likewise."

She sat down and opened a large black tote. From inside, she pulled out a pad of notepaper and a pen. After placing both on the table, she drew in a breath and turned her attention to him.

"I understand your sister is getting married."

"So she tells me." He smiled.

Madeline stiffened, then drew in a breath. "December 26? The Saturday after Christmas?"

He nodded.

"All right. So here's the thing. I work at Paper Moon. It's a bridal gown store. I'm the manager there. I work with brides every day. I handle the details of their gowns, veils and often shoes. I outfit the wedding party. Sometimes I have to act as referee between various family members. Grandma doesn't always approve of the bride's choice."

He'd seen enough reality TV to know that was true. But he had a feeling Madeline hadn't yet gotten to the point of their conversation. She had something to say and he was going to be patient until she got it out.

She looked at her blank pad of paper, then back at him. "I'm not a professional wedding coordinator. I'm not even an amateur one. I've seen a lot of weddings and my friend Dellina, who's an actual event planner, has offered to give me direction, but this isn't what I do for a living. Having said that, I'm happy to help you with this, if you'd like. Or you can bring in someone from Los Angeles or wherever. It's totally up to you."

Jonny couldn't remember the last time someone told him she couldn't do the job. Everyone generally overpromised and underdelivered. It was a fact of life. They wanted his money or the prestige of saying they worked for him. The former made sense. People had to make a living. But the latter genuinely flummoxed him. The fame might screw up his life, but it wasn't real. It was imposed on him. Underneath the big name on the billboard, he was just a guy doing a job. A really weird job, but still. There was nothing magical about his abilities. He wasn't saving the world. He was jumping out of planes and punching fake bad guys. Not the stuff of legends.

None of which was Madeline's problem, he thought, looking at her.

She was pretty enough. Her makeup was light and he would guess none of her features had been altered by the careful skill of a plastic surgeon. She was dressed in a simple black dress. The style was plain and didn't really suit her. No doubt she picked her clothes to blend in, rather than stand out. In her line of work, the bride would be the star.

"Just to confirm," he said, picking up his latte, "you've

never planned a wedding. You're open to having me hire someone else, but if I need your help, you'll be there."

"Yes."

"Okay, then. Ginger and I don't have any family, but her fiancé does. He'll have ten or twelve relatives attending. The rest of the guests will be Ginger's and Oliver's friends. As of my last conversation with my sister, we're at forty-four guests."

Madeline picked up her pen, then put it down. "Is this conversation or information?"

He thought about his sister. She was sweet and funny and, by far, the smartest person he knew. She wanted a small, quiet celebration. Simple. Ordinary. She would hate anything big or flashy. A wedding planner from LA would want to design an extravaganza. Something that could make her career. Jonny wanted Ginger to be happy. Nothing else.

Madeline Krug, wedding-gown store manager of Fool's Gold, California, would understand what Ginger wanted. And she had no portfolio to build at Ginger's expense.

"Information," he said firmly. "I want you to help me with my sister's wedding."

Madeline resisted the need to ask the obvious question. Why would anyone want her to plan a wedding?

Although it was possible the answer would be clear to someone who wasn't suffering from being so incredibly close to Jonny Blaze.

She was pleased that she was able to breathe. And her heart seemed to be working fine. Maybe it was because the moment was so surreal. Here she was in the town where she'd grown up, sitting across from Jonny Blaze.

Up close he was just as handsome as he was on-screen. His eyes were a beautiful shade of deep green and his hair was glossy and dark. She wondered if that was his natural color, because it had been light brown, blond and red for various roles.

He was broad-shouldered, with muscles. Thin, but not skinny. When he spoke, he sounded incredibly normal. She simply couldn't reconcile what was happening, although she was going to try to go with it. The alternative was to run screaming into the street and that didn't look attractive on anyone.

"What are you thinking?" he asked unexpectedly.

Madeline blinked. No way she could answer that question. Not directly at least.

"That you're a regular person."

He flashed her another smile. "Thanks for noticing. Some people don't."

"How strange. To go through life with people thinking they know you when they don't," she said without thinking. "It must be both good and bad."

"It is." He sipped his latte. "We should talk about your fee."

Madeline felt her eyes widen. "What? Fee? No. You're not paying me. This isn't a job. Mayor Marsha asked me to help out and I'm happy to."

He put down the drink and leaned toward her. He was so close she could see all the colors of green and gold in his irises. It was mesmerizing. As was he.

"You can't do this for nothing," he told her.

"Why not?"

She tried to control her breathing so she wouldn't start hyperventilating. The man was impossibly handsome. The line of his jaw, the shape of his mouth. She could sit here and shiver and stare all day long.

"You're doing a job."

"I'm helping out a fellow citizen. There's a difference." She drew in a slow breath. "I'm not doing this because you're Jonny Blaze. I'm doing this because you live here." She shrugged. "The store is quiet this time of year and I'm looking forward to seeing a wedding through from start to finish. Normally all I get to deal with is the wedding gown."

He didn't look convinced, but that didn't matter. There was no way he was going to pay her. That was just icky.

"Tell you what," she said with a grin. "You figure out what you think is a fair amount to pay me and then you can donate that amount to HERO—our local search and rescue program."

He studied her as if she weren't anything he'd encountered before. "You're a little strange."

"Just like the town?"

"Yes, and equally unexpected." He nodded slowly. "All right, Madeline. I accept your offer to help and I will make a generous contribution to your favorite charity."

"Deal. Now I should probably talk to your sister to get her thoughts about what we're doing."

"Good idea."

He gave her Ginger's email address and cell number.

"Set up a time to talk. If she's not in the lab, she's studying or working on her dissertation."

"Okay. I'll email her as soon as I get back to the office. Once she and I have spoken, I'll have a more clear idea of what she wants. Then I'll put some ideas together and you and I can talk about them."

"Great. I appreciate you helping me. I want Ginger to have the wedding of her dreams."

"Then we'll make that happen."

They both rose. She held out her hand to shake, re-alizing a half second too late that it might be a mistake. He took her hand in his and they shook. People did it thousands of times a day. Maybe millions.

But she'd never done it with Jonny Blaze, so was un-prepared for the hot, melty sparks that erupted all over her body. Or the way her chest got tight and her thighs tingled.

Lightning, she thought with amazement. The light-ning her mother had always told her about. The lightning that meant the women in her family had found *the one*.

No, she told herself firmly as she pulled back her hand. Not lightning. Star power. There was a very big differ-ence and she would do well to remember that.

❧ TWO ❧

JONNY PARKED HIS SUV NEAR the lake and walked the rest of the way into town for his meeting with Madeline. He found that when he was in Fool's Gold, he liked being out and walking around with everyone. The air was cool—they'd already had the first snowfall of the season. People were bundled up with scarves and jackets, but the extra layers and chill didn't keep them from greeting each other.

He'd been smiled at and wished a good day more times than he could count. It was nice. Regular. At least out here. In LA everyone would be driving, even if they only had to go three blocks, and in New York, each person was in his or her own personal bubble. He didn't have to worry about paparazzi. They'd shown up for about two days after he'd moved here. But once they'd realized there was nothing to report, they'd left him alone. Which was exactly how he liked it.

He'd spoken to his sister that morning. She'd had a good conversation with Madeline and was excited about her upcoming wedding.

He'd wondered if Ginger would ask Madeline about her credentials, but his sister had only raved about how Madeline understood exactly what she wanted. For his part, he needed a local connection because he wanted to use vendors from the area. While flying in someone from LA might be easier, working with Madeline gave him more control.

Ginger's wedding was important to him. Since their dad had died nearly a decade before, it had been Jonny and his sister. They looked out for each other. Seeing her get married would be great. He liked her fiancé. Oliver was a good guy. Just as smart and focused as Ginger. They did well together.

He crossed the street, heading for Paper Moon. He was meeting Madeline in her store. As he turned a corner, a woman walked up to him. She was a tall, attractive redhead.

"You're Jonny Blaze," she said as she stopped next to him. "I've been looking for you."

Talk about the inevitable, he thought, wondering if he had a pen with him. While it had taken longer here than most places, him being recognized and stopped was a part of celebrity life. Mostly he was fine with being asked for an autograph or picture even when he was between movies or publicity tours, like now. Because his fans didn't care if he was working or simply enjoying a few weeks off.

He glanced at the woman's left hand and saw a wedding band. Hopefully that meant she wasn't going to come on to him. Although it didn't always.

The fame thing was complicated. He had to admit, there were times when he liked not having to wait in line or always being able to get a table at a popular restaurant. But the downside could be dark, and for the most part he preferred to live privately.

"I'm Felicia Boylan," the woman continued. "I run the festivals here in town."

"Nice to meet you."

"Nice to meet you, as well." She offered him a quick smile. "We have a parade in town on Thanksgiving morning. Will you be here for the holiday?"

"I will." Ginger was going to be spending it with Oliver's family, so he was on his own.

For a second he worried this Felicia woman was inviting him to dinner. Not that he wouldn't enjoy some company, but he wasn't interested in hanging out with people he didn't know. Then the comment about her job, along with the parade, clicked into place and he got it.

She wanted him to be the grand marshal. He wondered who had gotten bumped when Felicia had found out he'd moved to the area. And while he appreciated the offer, he wasn't exactly a parade kind of guy. He would let her down gently, he told himself. No hard feelings and all that.

"Excellent. I heard you had a classic car. A 1956 Cadillac convertible. An El Dorado, I believe."

Her stare was intense, as if she wanted to be sure she got all her facts right.

"That's right," he said slowly.

"And it's red?"

He nodded.

The smile returned. "Perfect. I was hoping we could borrow it for the parade. The vehicle Mayor Marsha normally uses isn't working and it appears the parts won't arrive in time. I was hoping your car could be the backup. We have insurance. I would personally watch over your car. So can we borrow it for the parade?"

The car was in mint condition with white leather interior. He loved that car. But what he couldn't wrap his mind around was the fact that Felicia wanted *it*, rather than *him*, in the parade.

"You want to borrow my car," he confirmed.

"Yes. For the parade." She drew her eyebrows together. "You do know what a parade is, don't you? If not, I'm happy to explain."

"I have a basic idea of what's involved." The car. Huh. He never would have guessed that. "Okay. You're welcome to my car."

"Thank you. I'll be in touch to make arrangements."

With that, she hurried away. Jonny stared after her, then shook his head. He was the one who'd wanted to be treated like everyone else. He should be grateful only his car was going to be in the parade.

He continued walking and saw Paper Moon up ahead. The big front windows displayed wedding gowns along with shoes and veils. When he stepped into the store, he paused to glance around.

A few years ago he'd dated a set designer. From her he'd learned how seemingly insignificant details could set the mood or ruin the moment. That a misplaced lamp could produce awkward shadows and that furniture created movement.

Now he took in the high ceilings, the plush furniture, the elegant armoires and shelves. Everything directed the eye toward a kind of dais placed in front of a half circle of ten-foot-high mirrors. He would guess that customers stepped up in front of those mirrors and immediately became the center of attention. Practice for the spotlight of the big day, he thought.

To his left were racks of wedding gowns. An open doorway led to another room, also filled with dresses, but they were for the bridesmaids, he would guess.

"Jonny."

He turned and saw Madeline approaching. She was still dressed in black—this time a sweater and slim pants. Her hair was wavy, her makeup simple. She looked polished and capable. Reassuring, he thought. Brides would like that.

"Thanks for coming here," she said as she stopped in front of him. Humor brightened her blue eyes. "All this girlie stuff making you sweat?"

He chuckled. "Not even close. You forget, in my job I have to wear makeup."

"That's right. Then I won't feel guilty for asking you to visit my office."

"Don't. I like coming into town and this gave me an excuse." He looked at the dresses. "They're like costumes. A woman puts them on and becomes someone else for the day."

"I hadn't thought of it that way, but you're right. It is a costume for a rite of passage." She tilted her head as she smiled at him. "Although if I'm doing my job right, instead of becoming someone else, she becomes a better version of herself."

"Good for you."

She was smart, he thought. Easy to talk to. Both of which would be an asset in her career. She would have to get along with a lot of different types of people. Bend to them, find out what they wanted and make it happen.

It had been a long time since that had been his problem. Mostly people did what he wanted. More often than not, they anticipated his needs. After a while, it was easy to forget how to be normal, which was the reason he didn't have a personal assistant. One was always hired for him when he was filming, but the rest of the time, he made himself deal with stuff like grocery shopping and laundry.

"My office is this way." She pointed to a narrow hallway, then turned to lead the way.

He followed, his gaze dropping to the sway of her hips. As she moved, he found himself intrigued by the curve of her ass and the length of her legs. As he couldn't remember the last time he'd been even slightly tempted, he enjoyed the sensation of waking arousal.

On the bright side, that part of him wasn't dead. Something to remember when the nights got long.

Her office was small and utilitarian. No window—just a few file cabinets, a battered desk, her chair and two others for visitors. A plastic palm tree nestled close to pictures of an older couple, along with a man in his midforties. There was also a younger woman close to twenty. A younger sister, he would guess. And the man?

So much for his brief moment of fantasy, he thought as he pointed to the photos.

"Your husband?"

She turned, then shook her head. "I'm not married. That's my brother and his daughter, Jasmine. Those are my parents."

All good news, he thought. "Nice family."

"Thanks."

He settled in one of the visitor chairs. "How long have you owned the store?"

"What? I don't. I'm a partner. Isabel Hendrix owns most of it. She bought it from her parents a couple of years ago. It's been in her family over fifty years. Paper Moon is kind of a Fool's Gold tradition." Her voice turned wistful. "Nearly every little girl grows up imagining buying her dress here."

She smiled. "Luckily most of them end up doing just that. The other half of the business is women's clothing. A lot of regional designers who haven't been discovered yet. Isabel offered me a small percentage of the business to be paid out over several years. While I appreciate that, I'm putting in part of my salary to increase my ownership."

She wrinkled her nose. "Which is way more than you wanted to know. Sorry."

"Don't apologize. It's interesting. You're ambitious."

"In my tiny way, yes. I also want to earn my way in."

He liked that. Too many people wanted things given to them. He could appreciate that quirks of fate and just plain dumb luck could change everything. He was proof of that.

"That's why I'm excited about helping you with Ginger's wedding," she added. "It's a chance to learn something new."

Madeline couldn't tell if she sounded reasonably intelligent or had been reduced to babbling. Being this close to Jonny Blaze was still difficult. From a distance, she was able to maintain a clear line of thought. But when he was just on the other side of her small desk, well, her brain had other things on its mind.

It wasn't just that he was good-looking. In reality Fool's Gold had more than its share of handsome men wandering around. But he was different. She didn't know if it was the movie-star thing or a personality flaw or what. Her friend Felicia had once talked about the sociological aspects of hierarchy in the village. Something about having the biggest head.

No, that wasn't right. The most important person. But there was also something about a big head. Anyway, she would need to go talk to Felicia and get it figured out. She was pretty sure the theory would help her act more normal around Jonny Blaze.

Now she forced herself to remember why he was here—which wasn't to fill her afternoon with eye-candy moments. There was a wedding to organize and she was responsible for that.

"I spoke to Ginger," she said.

"She mentioned that. She liked you."

The unexpected comment momentarily flustered her. "I liked her, too. She's really nice. And excited about the wedding." Also dealing with school and the holidays and everything else. Just listening to all Ginger had going on had exhausted Madeline. "I made notes during our call. She confirmed what you said at our previous meeting. She wants a small, intimate, low-key wedding. The guest list is forty-four people and she swears it's not going to get any bigger."

"However big she wants it is fine with me," Jonny

said. "This is about Ginger and Oliver. She's my sister and what makes her happy, makes me happy."

A not uncommon sentiment from a big brother, yet nice to hear.

"The wedding is going to be at your ranch?" Madeline asked, checking her notes. "There's a barn?"

The lazy smile returned. "It's nicer than it sounds. The barn has been converted into a big, open space. We'll be able to fit in tables and decorations."

"What do you use it for?"

"I haven't decided. I knew I didn't need a place to house livestock."

"No desire to raise horses and cows?"

"Not this week. You'll probably want to come take a look at it."

Go to his house? Or his barn, but still. They were on the same property. She hoped she looked normal as she nodded and made a note. "That's a good idea. We can discuss decorations and table linens. I've already reserved the tables and chairs. I was worried they would all be set aside for other events. I wasn't sure if you had enough dishes and glasses, so I reserved those, as well."

"Good thinking." Concern drew his brows together. "I hadn't realized there was so much to organize. I'm glad we're working on this together."

His words made her tingle all over. Star power, she told herself. Nothing more than star power.

Madeline wrapped up her meeting with Jonny, then collected her handbag and walked toward the other side of the store. While wedding gowns would always be a part of Paper Moon, the retail clothing addition was doing well. Madeline found Isabel sorting through a shipment of handbags.

Her business partner, a tall, curvy blonde, smiled. "Is it time for lunch? Thank goodness. This has been one of those mornings. Only half of what I ordered got delivered and there was nearly a fistfight between two tourists who wanted the same jacket in the same size. I was afraid I was going to have to call for backup."

"You know where to find me," Madeline told her. "Rosalind is here most days, too. Between the three of us, we should be able to wrestle any unruly shopper into submission."

Isabel laughed. "Thank you for that. I feel better."

The words were appropriate, but there was something about the way Isabel said them. "Are you okay?"

"What? Of course. I'm fine. Why do you ask?"

"I'm not sure." There was something, Madeline thought, studying her friend. She just couldn't figure out what.

"You're feeling okay?" she asked.

Isabel had recently announced she was pregnant. As far as Madeline knew, everything was progressing normally.

Isabel put a hand on her belly. "Everything is going along as it should," she said firmly. "I'm healthy. Not to worry." She started for the back. "Give me one second and we'll head to Jo's."

Two minutes later they were walking to Jo's Bar, where they would meet their friends for lunch. The air was crisp. The first snow had already fallen and pretty much gone away. There were still a few piles left from clearing the sidewalks, but little else. Still, plenty more was on the way. While the first few snowfalls were always exciting, by month two of shoveling, Madeline knew she would be ready for spring. Still, it would be wonderful to have a white Christmas.

They ducked into Jo's Bar. The place catered to women and was decorated with flattering paint colors, good lighting. There were plenty of healthy choices on the menu. Today the TVs were tuned to either a shopping channel or a show on HGTV.

Madeline saw that Shelby and Destiny had already claimed a table. She waved at her friends, then led the way over.

"Hey, you," Shelby said, coming to her feet and hugging Madeline. She greeted Isabel, then moved so Madeline could say hi to a more-pregnant-by-the-day Destiny.

"You're growing," Madeline said with a laugh. "And glowing. Isabel, this is in your future."

"If only," Isabel said with a sigh. "I'll never look that good when I'm six months along."

"Don't be too nice to me," Destiny told them. "I'm very hormonal these days. I'll start crying."

"We don't want that," Shelby, a petite blonde, told her teasingly.

The two women smiled at each other. While Shelby and Madeline were close, Shelby and Destiny were sisters-in-law. Destiny had married Shelby's brother—former Olympic skier Kipling Gilmore—the previous summer. No one had known they were even seeing each other until the surprise wedding. Talk about keeping a secret.

Something Madeline was finally experiencing herself, she thought happily. Not that working for Jonny Blaze was as exciting as an illicit romance, but still. She knew that she was going to have to tell Isabel—what with her having to be gone from the shop from time to time. But that was for later. Right now she was keeping the information to herself. Mostly because she and Jonny hadn't discussed if it was public or not. Until she confirmed that he was okay with her mentioning it to her business partner, she wasn't saying a word.

The door opened and Patience, Taryn and Consuelo walked in. Or rather Taryn and Consuelo walked. Patience waddled, with her second child due the first week of January. The three women headed to their table.

Madeline loved her lunches out with her friends. The number and faces were always changing, but they had friendship in common. Today's group was eclectic, as always. Patience owned Brew-haha, the local coffee shop in town, Phoebe was a recent transplant from LA who was now a rancher's wife, Taryn ran a PR firm and Consuelo was an instructor at the bodyguard school.

Isabel looked at Taryn and shook her head. "I see you're back to your skinny self. Didn't you just have a baby last Tuesday?"

"I had Bryce in July," the violet-eyed brunette said with a grimace. "And I've been sweating in the gym every day for the past four months. I've had to lift weights. It's awful. So you don't get to be mad at me. I've earned my way back into my clothes."

Isabel stuck out her tongue and the rest of the women laughed.

"It feels good to be back to where I was," Taryn said.

Destiny rested her hand on her growing belly. "I look forward to it."

"Sing it, sister," Patience said.

Madeline was sure most women would agree with them, but she had to admit to a little disappointment. It seemed to her that having a baby should be transformative. That you shouldn't just slip back into your old life. Although she doubted carrying around an extra five or ten pounds was the right way to mark the occasion. She just knew that if she was lucky enough to fall in love and get married and have kids, she wanted the experience to change her.

Jo came by and took their orders. Conversation flowed easily. Phoebe mentioned hearing from Maya and Del, who were in China. That was followed by everyone admitting they had no idea how the Chinese celebrated the holidays, or if they did at all.

As people talked, Madeline became aware of Isabel fidgeting in her seat. She leaned close to her business partner.

"I know I keep asking this, but are you okay?"

Isabel surprised her by hugging her. "You're a good person, you know that, right?"

Madeline studied her. "Are you crying?"

"What Destiny has is contagious." Isabel cleared her throat, then sighed. "I have an announcement."

The table quieted. Isabel looked at them all. "I'm pregnant."

Consuelo frowned. "Did you hit your head? Do you have a concussion? We all know you're pregnant. If you hadn't told me, I'd still know. Ford tells me every single day. If I didn't like you so much, I would kill him because he's annoying."

A statement that from anyone else might be cause for alarm, but was exactly how Consuelo thought and talked.

Isabel seemed to brace herself. "I didn't hit my head. It's just… I had my ultrasound and…" She held up her hand. "I'm fine. I'm doing well. Too well. Because… I'm having triplets."

There was a moment of silence followed by loud cheers and calls of congratulations.

Madeline took in the news. She knew Isabel's husband, Ford, had triplet sisters, so it wasn't a complete surprise that she would be having multiples. It was just, well, Madeline had thought they were friends. That working together had brought them closer. Even though she'd asked, Isabel hadn't told her the news privately.

Madeline reminded herself that the information was

Isabel's to share and she shouldn't take the slight personally. It was just—

"Don't be mad," Isabel whispered. "I couldn't tell
you."

"Okay," Madeline said slowly, still not sure why.

"It's just… I was scared. I'm going to need you so
much and it's not fair, but without you, I can't keep the
business going."

Madeline hugged her. "You're an idiot."

"I know."

"Of course I'll help."

"You swear?"

"Try to get me to stop. I love you."

"I love you, too. You're the best business partner ever."

Madeline laughed. "You say that like it's news."

While the rest of the country seemed to jump from
Halloween to Christmas, in Fool's Gold the tradition of
giving thanks was embraced. Jonny saw gourds and straw
baskets, every form of turkey from paper to ceramic.
There were harvest garlands and fall-colored bunting
and plenty of pilgrims. Hokey but nice.

He wasn't sure how the transition to Christmas was
going to happen, but it would have to be nearly an overnight thing. There was a town Christmas tree light-

ing scheduled this coming Saturday, only two days after Thanksgiving.

He crossed the street and headed into Paper Moon. He could see Madeline up on the dais, with a bride. The young woman was maybe twenty, with brown hair and glasses. She reminded him a little of Ginger, with her earnest expression.

The dress had a big skirt, like something a Disney princess would wear. It suited her youth, he thought, then held in a grin. Next thing he knew he would be discussing makeup and shoes. Talk about a way to frighten off guy friends. His buddy Shep would sure have something to say about any discussion that girlie. For now, Jonny was safe. Shep was on loan to the search and rescue program in Yosemite and wouldn't be back until after the holidays.

A tall, blonde woman walked up to him. She studied him for a second, as if trying to place him. He saw the exact moment she realized who he was. To her credit, she barely blinked.

"Good afternoon," she said. "I'm Isabel Hendrix. May I help you?"

Now it was his turn to be startled. If the woman knew who he was, why didn't she know why he was here? He glanced from her to Madeline, who was hugging the young bride. The girl stepped off the dais and headed for the dressing room. Madeline followed her down the stairs, then walked over to join them.

"Hi," she said. "Did we have an appointment?"

A polite way of pointing out he was interrupting her workday. She stood up for herself. He liked that.

"I had a couple of ideas I wanted to talk to you about. When you have a free moment."

"Sure. I'll be about ten minutes, if you want to wait."

"Your office?"

Isabel glanced between them. "You two obviously know what you're doing. I'll head back to my side of the store."

She gave Madeline a look that clearly stated they would be talking later.

The promised ten minutes later, Madeline joined him. "How can I help you?" she asked as she settled behind her desk.

"You didn't tell her."

"What?"

"Your business partner. You didn't say you were working with me."

She shifted in her seat, then waved a hand. "I didn't know if I should, so I erred on the side of discretion. This is your private business. I don't talk about my brides with anyone. Not in any detail. I might ask for opinions on a dress or get suggestions, but what happens here is personal. Planning a wedding falls under the same category."

He could appreciate someone who respected privacy. "You can tell your business partner and anyone you'd like that you're helping me."

"Good, because I'll have to say something what with you showing up here and all."

"Should I have worn a disguise?"

"Maybe a fedora."

He chuckled. "Not sure I own one of those."

Madeline was dressed in her usual black, with her hair pulled back. She had on red lipstick. It was kind of sexy and, when combined with the prim cut of her blouse, gave her that naughty librarian look. He'd always been a sucker for librarians.

"You wanted to talk about the wedding?" she asked.

"Ice sculptures."

"Excuse me?"

"I was thinking ice sculptures to line the main driveway to the house and the walkway to the barn. Flowers in vases, maybe a few snowflakes for the holiday season. Just to make it more festive."

Madeline considered his words. "I never would have thought of them, but sure. I can run the idea past Ginger.

They'd add a nice touch. Also give some visual interest when people looked outside. Would you light them?"

"Of course."

"That could be really pretty." She pulled out a folder and made some notes. "I'm putting together information to email her tonight. I'll include this. And while I have you here, if you have the time, I have a couple of things I'd like you to look at."

"Sure thing."

It was nearly noon. He thought about asking if she wanted to have lunch with him. Because he enjoyed Madeline's company. Plus, the whole red-lip, buttoned-collar thing was working for him.

But then what? Getting involved with him was a nightmare. Someone always leaked the information to a tabloid and then it went to hell. In a town like Fool's Gold, there weren't going to be any secrets. Someone was bound to know someone who knew a guy who made his living taking pictures.

Jonny had been down that road before and it never ended well. He knew he was lucky. He made a lot of money at a job he really liked. It had allowed him to take care of his sister. But there was a price for fame, and sometimes it was one he didn't want to have to pay.

She handed over several sheets of paper. "Catering

ideas. I've been talking to Ana Raquel and I've marked her suggestions for what is the most popular. One of the challenges is the time of year—we can't always get all the seasonal options."

"We can fly in any fresh produce."

Madeline's blue eyes danced with amusement. "I'm sure we can," she said gently. "Ana Raquel is more concerned about not having a holiday-based meal. People will have been eating turkey and prime rib already. It's all heavy food. Her idea was to go for something lighter. Maybe even tropical. In contrast with the weather. Grilled fish and lots of finger foods."

Something he'd never considered. He knew that Oliver's family did a traditional turkey dinner on Christmas Eve and then had prime rib on Christmas Day. Exactly what the chef had said.

"They both like Mexican food," he said slowly as he scanned the suggestions. "What about combining that with tropical?" He pointed to the Coconut Popcorn Shrimp with Mango Lime Salsa. "Like this. They'd enjoy that a lot. Ginger wants casual and easy. Food like that would mean giving her what she's looking for."

"You're a good brother," Madeline said unexpectedly.

"I want Ginger to be happy."

"But you know stuff about her. That's nice. I have an

older brother. While I adore him and I know he'd be here in a heartbeat if I needed him, he has no idea if I like Mexican food or not."

"You're forgetting I took care of Ginger for a few years. I cooked and everything. I know exactly what she'll eat."

She studied him. "I'm trying to picture you in an apron."

He chuckled. "Never wore one of those."

"I'll talk to Ana Raquel and have her put together a menu combining tropical and Mexican foods. She makes a Black Bean Soup with Lime Cream that is to die for."

"Then we need that for sure."

Madeline made some notes. "It's Thanksgiving tomorrow, so let's say by Tuesday of next week? Are you going to be around?"

He nodded. "I'm driving to San Francisco this afternoon to have dinner with Ginger, then I'm heading back."

"Which means the timing is perfect." She pulled out another folder, then handed him several wedding invitations. "These are all the samples I could pull together on such short notice. If you don't like any of them, I'll get some more."

He laid out the invitations. They were all on thick card

stock. Several had a picture of the couple and he immediately dismissed those. While they were nice enough,
there wasn't time to get a photo taken.

"Which do you like?" he asked.

Madeline knew that she was helping with his sister's
wedding, but it was still strange to be asked her opinion on something like wedding invitations. Now if it
had been a veil, she would have been more comfortable with her choice. Still, she stood and leaned over the
desk. She'd looked at the samples as they'd come in and
already had a few favorites.

"These are nice," she said, pointing. "This one is a
layered package, with different cards tucked into one envelope. You can do the invitation on one card, provide
information on where to stay on another, have a map to
your place."

She tapped another one. "I'll admit it. I'm a sucker
for laser cutting. I think the lace effect on the paper is
spectacular, but hey, I sell wedding gowns for a living.
If I didn't revel in lace, I'd be in the wrong profession."

He laughed. "Good point."

He considered her choices, then pulled out one that
had a vintage feel and was cut to look like an unrolled

scroll. "I like this one. I'll take her all three and she can pick one tonight. I'll get them ordered first thing."

"Would you send me the confirmation when you do?" she asked, sitting back down and making a note on a pad of paper. "That way I can move it from the to-do list to the pending list."

"There's a pending list?"

"Yes, and a completed list, although, so far, that's blank."

"Once the menus are finalized, you can move that over."

She sighed. "You have no idea how much I'm looking forward to that happening." She wrote a couple more notes, then closed her folder. "That's all I have. If you're going to be busy with Ginger, I can order the invitations, once she chooses the one she wants."

He was a famous guy. He had to have places to go and people to see.

"I'll do it." He leaned back in his chair. "Won't you have family over the holidays?"

Madeline smiled. "I will. My parents have already flown in. As we speak, my mother is baking in my kitchen."

"Is that good or bad?"

"It's wonderful. She'll make cookies and brownies and cakes. I'll gain five pounds and every one is worth it."

"Nice," he said. "How many in the family?"

"I have one brother and a niece. Robbie lost his wife to cancer several years ago." The whole family had been devastated, Madeline thought, remembering the sadness of it all. "We've always been close, which I'm hoping helped them." She shook off the memories.

"My parents are older. My mom had Robbie ten months after she got married, but she couldn't get pregnant a second time. They'd pretty much given up when I came along." She thought about all the stories she'd been told. "Robbie was seventeen when Mom announced she was pregnant and eighteen when I was born. He admits he was pretty horrified to realize his parents were still having sex."

"So you were a surprise."

"Yes, but they swear I was a good one."

"You had to be."

She laughed. "I'm sure I was a challenge, but my parents were always there for me. We have great traditions and I'm really close with my niece. Jasmine is only eight years younger than me. We text all the time. She's going to die when she finds out you're in town."

"You haven't told her?" He held up a hand. "Don't answer that. Madeline, I appreciate you're respecting my privacy, but you can tell your family. Only if you want. I don't expect to be a topic of conversation."

She laughed. "That would be kind of weird. Although we're always looking for new traditions. You could be one."

"Thanks, but no."

She wondered what he did for his traditions. She would guess there had been years when he'd been away on movie shoots, or whatever they called it, over the holidays. Times when he couldn't get home.

He'd mentioned that he was seeing Ginger that night, but what about tomorrow? Would he be alone for Thanksgiving? And if he was...

She dismissed the thought before it could fully form. On what planet would she be inviting Jonny Blaze to her house for anything? She couldn't begin to imagine him sitting next to her mother or father. They would have nothing to talk about. It was too strange and he might think she was interested in him. So no. He was a rich, famous guy. He had a thousand places he could go. She was crazy to think about him being lonely on Thanksgiving.

He glanced at his watch. "If there's nothing else, I'm going to get on the road."

"Drive safely," she told him.

"I will." He collected the three sample invitations, then stood. "We'll talk after the holiday?"

"Absolutely. Happy Thanksgiving."

"Same to you."

❦3 THREE ❦

MADELINE WAITED UNTIL JONNY LEFT to go find Isabel. Her business partner was sorting through inventory. They'd been discussing putting a few items online to see if they could start selling across the country. Several tourists had expressed interest in having access to the clothes without having to fly back to town.

"So, that was interesting," she said as she walked into the storeroom.

Isabel looked up and smiled. "If you're trying to illustrate that keeping the information about the triplets to myself wasn't my best idea, point taken."

Madeline walked to her and touched her arm. "That wasn't it at all. Mayor Marsha came to see me and asked me to help Jonny plan his sister's wedding. Dellina's busy, and as it's only going to be a small event at his house, it seemed as if I couldn't mess it up."

Isabel winced. "Mayor Marsha asked you personally?"

"Uh-huh."

"Then you didn't have a choice." Her friend's smile turned impish. "So, you're working in close proximity to the gorgeous, muscled Jonny Blaze. Does he know about your mad crush on him?"

"No, and he doesn't need to."

"I'm not so sure about that. Is it fun? Are you having trouble breathing?"

"A little," Madeline admitted. "It's getting easier. I can go a whole three minutes without hyperventilating. Give me another two weeks and I'll last for an hour without remembering who he is."

"Is he nice?"

Madeline thought about their brief meetings and how he obviously loved his sister. "He is, and way more normal than I would have thought. He's just a regular guy."

"Seriously?"

Madeline grinned. "Okay, maybe that's too strong, but he's not that different. He doesn't act like a movie star."

"Any tingles?"

"Plenty and I'm not the least bit concerned. Look at who he is. Tingles come with the territory. They're about star power, not the man."

"You're sure? Because you're great and he'd be lucky

to have you, but I'm not sure he'd be happy with a small-town girl."

"Me, either." As if, Madeline thought humorously. "Although if he wanted to tie himself in red ribbon and be waiting under my Christmas tree, I wouldn't say no."

"I doubt there are many women who would. 'Dear Santa, all I want for Christmas is Jonny Blaze.'"

Madeline laughed. "You've been reading my email." She glanced at the clock on the wall. It was nearly noon, which meant she needed to be going.

"Are they here?" Isabel asked, following her gaze.

"I'm guessing my mom already has the oven going," Madeline said happily.

"Tell everyone hi from me and we'll see you tomorrow. About seven?"

"Whatever works for you."

Madeline gave her business partner a hug, then returned to the wedding gown side of the store. Rosalind would work until three, then close things down for the holiday. Madeline was leaving early to go meet her family.

As they did each Thanksgiving, her mother and father, brother and niece returned to Fool's Gold. Like migrating birds, she thought with a grin as she grabbed her handbag and called out that she was leaving.

Once she was outside, she breathed in the chilly air. It even smelled like a holiday. The streets were more crowded than usual, with people running last-minute errands. There were plenty of tourists, as well, in town for the festivities.

The holiday season bonanza of activities started with the Thanksgiving parade tomorrow afternoon. That was followed by the official tree lighting on Saturday and so on, right up through New Year's. Madeline enjoyed all of it. She was on the committee for the Live Nativity, which was exactly how it sounded, live animals and all.

For the most part the committee work was easy enough. There were some unusual choices such as Priscilla the elephant and her pony, Reno. The only disagreement had been when someone had suggested a toy poodle stand in for the Baby Jesus. But what was life without controversy?

Not that she had to worry about her committee today. Instead, she would be spending time with her family.

She walked the ten blocks to her small house, then smiled when she saw the rental car in her driveway. Her parents had flown in from their place in Florida while her brother and niece would be arriving from O'Hare. Jasmine was a sophomore at Northwestern, while Robbie, Madeline's brother, was a pediatrician in Saint Paul.

She ran up the three steps to her porch, then opened the front door and stepped inside.

"I'm home," she called.

Her parents stepped out of the kitchen and hurried toward her. "My darling Maddie," her mother said, her arms open, her smile welcoming. "How are you?"

Her dad grinned. "She looks good, Loretta. She looks good."

Madeline was captured in their embrace. She hugged them back, letting the love wash over her.

She'd been lucky, she thought to herself. Lucky to be born into such a loving family. While she'd always known that her parents were older than her friends', she'd been okay with that. Loretta and Joseph had nurtured her, encouraging her to believe in herself and follow her dreams. The only flaw in their plan had been how long it had taken Madeline to figure out what she wanted to do with her life.

It hadn't helped to have such a successful older brother. By the time she entered first grade, Robbie was already in medical school. But he'd always taken time to pay attention to her, and while they hadn't grown up together, they'd been close.

Now she smiled at her parents. "How was your flight?"

"Excellent," her father said. "Your mother fretted the whole way."

"I didn't fret," Loretta said with a laugh. "I thought they were flying too slow. I couldn't wait to get here."

Her parents had arrived in Sacramento late the previous evening. With her dad pushing seventy-five, they preferred to wait until morning to make the drive to Fool's Gold.

"Did you check into the hotel?" Madeline asked. "If you didn't, you can still change your minds and stay here."

Her mother touched her cheek. "You're sweet to offer, but you need your space and so do we."

Because Madeline's house was charming, but only had two bedrooms and a single bathroom. She'd chosen it because the living area was large, as was the kitchen. But the spare room was practically closet-size.

"I'd sleep on the futon," she pointed out.

"We're fine at the lodge," her father said, hugging her again. "We always run into old friends there."

They went into the kitchen. Her mother already had peanut butter cookies in the oven and fresh coffee in the pot.

"Did you check everything?" Madeline asked. "I went

over the list a couple of times and I'm pretty sure it's all here."

Her mother laughed. "You did an excellent job. I did check and you remembered everything."

The Krug family had a Thanksgiving tradition. The parade, followed by dinner, followed by an open house that lasted well into the night. Friends and neighbors dropped in to visit. There were cakes and cookies and pies, along with good conversation and plenty of laughter. It was one of her favorite memories from childhood.

When her parents had moved to Florida, the tradition had been dropped. Madeline had gone to visit them for the holiday. But when she'd bought her place a couple of years ago, her parents had wanted to spend Thanksgiving in Fool's Gold and she'd found herself hosting the annual open house.

"I brought you something," her mother said, going to her handbag and pulling out a red box. "For Christmas."

Madeline stared at the box and knew exactly what was inside. They were a family tradition and had been on the Christmas dinner table her entire life.

Her mother's smile faded. "Was I wrong to bring them? Are you sad? Oh, Joseph, did we make a mistake, booking the cruise over Christmas?"

Madeline took the small box and opened it. She pulled

out the cardinal salt and pepper shakers and placed them on the counter. "They're beautiful. Thank you for bringing them to me. I'll use them, I promise. As for you making a mistake, you didn't. You're going to have a good time."

"But you'll be by yourself." Her mother's brows drew together. "We worry about you."

Because for the first time they wouldn't be spending Christmas together. Robbie and Jasmine would be with Robbie's in-laws and her parents had booked a holiday cruise with two other couples.

When they'd first told Madeline, she'd felt a little twinge. But then she'd reminded herself that they'd worked hard all their lives and they deserved to enjoy their retirement.

"I'll be fine," she told them. "I have lots of friends. You know that. The big question is which invitation to accept for dinner." Her parents didn't look that reassured.

She searched for something else to say—something that would reassure them. She brightened. "Besides, I'm going to be so swamped. I'm planning a wedding."

"Who's getting married? Why didn't I know one of your friends had gotten engaged?"

Madeline chuckled. "Mom, you have to brace yourself. I'm not helping a friend. Do you know who Jonny Blaze is?"

"The actor?" her mother asked.

"I enjoy his movies," her father added. "*Amish Revenge* is one of my favorites. We have the DVD."

"He's getting married?" Her mother shook her head. "I don't understand."

"It's not him, it's his sister."

Madeline explained about Mayor Marsha and the request, along with the subsequent conversations. "You can't tell anyone," she added. "It's a private thing."

"Of course," her mother said. "You're very sweet to help him out." Her mouth curved into a teasing smile. "Is he just as handsome in person?"

"You know it."

Her father cleared his throat. "Loretta, do I have to worry about you?"

His wife laughed. "Hardly. Jonny Blaze is young enough to be my son."

"That doesn't matter. You're a beautiful woman and he'd be lucky to have you. What I want to know is how hard I have to fight to keep you."

Their teasing warmed Madeline from the inside out. Her parents were loving, in love and just plain good people.

She worried about them because of their ages. She wasn't ready to lose either of them. But they were both healthy and Robbie assured her they should live well into their nineties. While she would like them around forever, she would take what she could get.

A car pulled into the driveway. Her mother clapped and her father headed to the front door.

"Right on time," Madeline said, just as excited to see the rest of her family.

The next few minutes passed in a blur of greetings and hugs as Robbie and Jasmine were welcomed into the house. Flights were discussed and the cardinal salt and pepper shakers were cooed over.

By the time all that was done, Madeline found herself in the kitchen with her niece. Jasmine pulled up a bar stool and scooped batter onto waiting cookie sheets.

"I don't know, Maddie," the twenty-one-year-old admitted. "Dad doesn't say anything, but I can feel the pressure."

"Your dad wants you to be happy."

"He wants me to be a pediatrician."

"Probably, but he'll settle for you being happy."

Because while Jasmine had said she was interested in medicine, her decision to focus on radiology was different than her initial plan to follow in her father's footsteps. Jasmine's mother had died of breast cancer.

Her death had changed them all. Jasmine especially. She'd decided to focus her sadness in a productive way. Something Robbie would have already guessed.

"He loves you," Madeline pointed out. "He'll be fine."

Jasmine, a blue-eyed blonde like the rest of the Krug women, wrinkled her nose. "Maybe you could talk to him."

"Maybe you could talk to him yourself."

"Why do I have to act like an adult?"

"It builds character and you might want to have the skill later, so it's good to practice."

Jasmine laughed. "If you insist."

"I do."

Robbie walked into the kitchen. He was nearly six feet, with light brown hair that was going gray at the temples. He smiled when he spotted them talking.

"How are my two favorite girls?"

"Good," Madeline said. "I think it's going to snow."

"I hope so. It's so fun here when it snows."

Madeline grinned at her brother. "I would think you'd get enough snow at home."

Robbie snagged one of the cooling cookies and took a bite. "It's different here."

"Magical," his daughter said.

"I don't think I'd go that far, but close." He turned to Madeline. "You okay with the holiday plans? You can come with Jasmine and me if you want."

Madeline appreciated the concern for what would be her first Christmas without her family. "I'll be fine. I've already talked to Mom. I have friends and plenty to keep me busy. Don't worry."

"Grandma Pat said it was okay," Jasmine added. "Just so you know."

Grandma Pat was Robbie's mother-in-law and Jasmine's maternal grandmother. "Tell her thank you, but I'm staying in Fool's Gold." She had work and a wedding to plan. There was also the slight chance she might be caught under some mistletoe with a very handsome Jonny Blaze.

Around noon on Thanksgiving, Jonny drove into town for the parade. He was curious to see the festivities, not to mention cheer on his car. He wasn't sure Mayor Marsha was a 1956 El Dorado kind of gal, but who was he to judge?

He was surprised by the number of people already lining the streets. It took him a while to find parking and then he had to walk nearly a mile back to the parade route. He passed lots of families. Parents with kids in strollers and even parents with teenagers. He would have expected the older kids to head off to be with their friends, but from what he could see, they were pretty willing to stay with the old folks. A few people smiled and called out a greeting. He had a feeling that was about the day and not him, which he liked.

The temperature was brisk—probably the midthirties. Cold but not unbearable. The sky was clear, but he would swear he could smell the promise of snow. On the corner, Brew-haha had set up a kiosk with mugs of cocoa and coffee. Next to that was a food cart that sold all kinds of Thanksgiving-shaped cookies. Turkeys and pumpkins and Pilgrim hats. He got a coffee and a couple of cookies, then strolled around in the crowd.

There was plenty of conversation. He heard snippets of different discussions on everything from the favorite part of the parade to what side dishes a certain mother-in-law expected her new daughter-in-law to make. When the faint notes of music drifted toward them, the crowd went quiet, then began to cheer.

He turned with everyone else, eager to catch his first glimpse of this small-town parade.

"Oh. My. God. You're Jonny Blaze. I can't believe it.

What are you doing here? Do you live here? Is it really you? Can I have an autograph and take a picture?"

It took a second for the frantic words to register. Jonny turned and saw a woman in her thirties staring at him. She was holding a toddler and there was a slightly older girl hanging on to her free hand. He knew he'd never seen her before and guessed she was a tourist in town for the long weekend.

The woman stared at him, then nodded. "It's you. I can't believe it. Mike, hurry. It's Jonny Blaze. You need to take our picture. This is amazing. Can we kiss, because wow, would I like to kiss you."

This happened all the time. He knew exactly what to do, how to establish boundaries. He'd been doing it for years. Only in the past few weeks, he'd forgotten what it was like to have the public intruding into his life. So he wasn't prepared and in the seconds it took him to figure out what he was supposed to say—beyond "Hell, no, we can't kiss"—the woman was moving in for her picture.

"You're going to feel really foolish in a minute."

The voice came from behind him, then a woman who had to be in her seventies pushed in front of him.

"I know what you're thinking," she continued cheerfully. "That he's that movie star Jonny something, right? Happens all the time." The old lady slapped him on his upper arm. "This is my no-good grandson. He can't hold a job to save his soul. My daughter is pulling her hair out, let me tell you. Now he's not the brightest bulb in the chandelier, but he's learned how to clean out gutters. You have some work he could do? He's honest and he's cheap."

The woman holding the baby took a giant step back. "You're not Jonny Blaze? And you were going to kiss me? I don't think so. Yuck." She rolled her eyes. "Why would I want to kiss a stranger?"

My point exactly, Jonny thought as the woman and her family hurried away.

He turned to the old lady. "Thank you."

"You're welcome. I saw them moving in for the kill and figured you could use some help."

"I'm usually better than that."

She shrugged. "It's okay. Everyone gets to have an off day. I'm Gladys, by the way."

"Jonny Blaze."

She grinned. "Like I don't know that. Nice to meet you officially. You're very handsome."

He laughed. "Okay, don't get scary."

She winked. "I know things. You'd be amazed."

"I probably would be. And then you'd dump me and break my heart."

"Very possibly." She eyed him speculatively. "I do have a great-niece who's single. Actually, Nancee's in a relationship with a no-good jerk, but does she listen?"

"They never do."

She motioned to someone he couldn't see. "I'm leaving you with protection, seeing as you're woefully unprepared to take care of yourself."

He turned and saw Madeline walking toward them. Gladys quickly explained what had happened.

Madeline turned to him. "Are you okay?"

She was genuinely concerned. He could read it in her blue eyes. Talk about strange—people didn't look out for him, they took from him. He was expected to be the one to provide. If he needed help, he hired security.

She was dressed in a bright red coat that matched her lip gloss. A matching scarf was wrapped around her neck and she had on mittens. Nothing overtly sexy, yet he found the outfit appealing. And very Fool's Gold.

"I'm fine," he told her. "Just an overly zealous tourist. Gladys shut her down."

"Gladys is good at doing that. But brace yourself. She's going to want payback."

"She already mentioned us sleeping together," he said, telling himself she really had been joking.

"If only it would stop there." Madeline glanced around.

"You're a sitting duck out like this. Come on." She pointed down the street. "You can hang out with my family. We're small in number, but mighty in spirit."

He wanted to say he could take care of himself—that he wasn't some dweeb who needed protecting. Only he liked her looking out for him. It was strange, but kind of nice. Like the town, he thought as he walked with her.

Madeline stopped in front of an older couple. Jonny remembered what she'd said about being a late-in-life surprise for her parents.

"Mom, Dad, this is Jonny Blaze. Jonny, my parents, Joseph and Loretta Krug."

If the older Krugs were surprised, they didn't let on. They both greeted him, then shook his hand.

"No relationship to the French Krugs," her father said with a wink.

It took Jonny a second to make the connection. "The champagne guy," he said.

"That's the one."

"I wouldn't mind being related to a champagne baron," a tall, younger man said.

Jonny took in the similarities between Joseph and the man standing next to him, then held out his hand. "You must be Madeline's brother."

"Robbie. Nice to meet you. And this is my daughter, Jasmine."

"Hi," the young woman said with a smile. "Wow, you really are Jonny Blaze."

"It's just a rumor," he told her.

The music got louder and everyone turned toward the street. He could see a banner carried by members of the high school drill team. Behind them was his car with Mayor Marsha sitting on the open back, her feet firmly planted on the rear seat.

"She's beautiful," Madeline teased. "Does it hurt to see her in public like that?"

"No. Better for her to be admired by all."

Robbie moved next to them. "We're talking about the car, right? Not that I don't love Mayor Marsha, but words like that would make me really uncomfortable."

Madeline linked arms with her brother. "Don't worry. Jonny is already spoken for. Gladys has made her play for him."

Robbie slapped him on the back. "You're a braver man than me."

"Gee, thanks."

Behind the car with the mayor was the marching band. Jonny wondered if the good mayor had thought to invest in earplugs, because the music was loud. Then he remembered this wasn't her first rodeo. She was California's longest-serving mayor and he would guess there was very little she wasn't prepared for.

After the marching band came the floats. Some were expected—like the decorated fire truck. Others surprised him. There was a giant plastic polar bear, all decked out for the holidays. Of course, that was nothing when compared with an actual live elephant, dressed like Santa.

Loretta, Madeline's mother, moved next to him. "Before you ask," she murmured, "they keep it on with Velcro. Several women in town banded together to make the costume. The tricky part is getting it on her. Not that she doesn't cooperate. She does. But she's a big girl."

He nodded, wondering how on earth an elephant came to be dressed as Santa in a parade. Of course, she was trailed by a pony and a goat, both in elf costumes, so hey.

Loretta leaned close. "What are your plans for dinner? Would you like to join us? Before you answer, I'll tell you that it's just family for the meal. Maddie and I have been cooking since yesterday and everything is delicious, if I do say so myself. After dinner, there's an open house. Our friends and neighbors stop by to welcome in the holiday season."

He thought about the big, empty house waiting for him back at his ranch. He'd come to Fool's Gold looking for privacy and solitude. After having found both, he had to admit that the nights could get a little long and lonely.

"I'd like that," he told her. "Thank you."

She patted his arm. "Good. Friends are always welcome at our table."

She moved back to stand next to her husband. Jonny glanced from her to the man at her side and wondered how his life would have been different if he hadn't lost his mother when Ginger was born and his father over a decade ago. Family was important. He knew that Ginger kept him grounded. When he wasn't sure what decision to make about a project, he picked the one he knew would make her proud. Without someone to love, a person didn't have an anchor.

Madeline smiled at him. "Everything okay?"

"Your mom invited me to dinner. Hope it's okay I said yes."

Her smile was immediate and welcoming. "Brace yourself. It's loud."

"Small in number but mighty in spirit?"

She laughed. "Exactly."

✤ FOUR ✤

"Madeline knew that in a few weeks her life would return to normal and she would look back and wonder if any of this had actually happened. But until then, she would simply go with it and tell herself that washing dishes with movie star Jonny Blaze was just one in a series of memories she would bore people with when she was eighty.

As she'd already told him twice he wasn't expected to help, she didn't bother saying it again. Instead, she passed him a clean casserole dish to dry. The dishwasher was chugging away, the leftovers were already put in the refrigerator and a final batch of sugar cookies was in the oven. The warm, sweet scent filled the kitchen, overriding the last delicious whiff of turkey and gravy.

"I'm so full," she admitted as she reached for the china gravy boat. "I hope I still fit in my clothes tomorrow."

"Do you get a lot of customers on Black Friday?" he asked.

"Not really. It's not a big shopping day for brides-to-be. Thanksgiving doesn't bring out the proposals. Christmas and New Year's are different, so in January I'm busy."

"Are you their first stop?" he asked, putting the dry dish on the counter next to the others.

They'd already finished the wineglasses and serving dishes. She emptied the dishpan and rinsed it, then peeled off her gloves. She leaned against the sink.

"While it's not all about the dress, it's an easy thing to start looking for," she told him. "Going to look at flowers or studying menus isn't exactly the same. Trying on a dress gives the bride immediate feedback. She can see how she's going to look on her wedding day. Tasting a small piece of cake isn't the same as seeing the whole thing, life size."

She smiled. "It's fun to see them, all excited, flashing the ring. I guess it's one of the last rites of passage and I enjoy being a part of that."

Something he couldn't possibly be interested in, she thought. But even as she thought about changing the subject, he moved a little closer, as if listening intently.

"What's the best part?" he asked.

"I'm not sure what it is for them, but for me it's when

the bride knows she's found the right dress. I can tell by the look on her face. Everything just feels right."

Like this moment, she though hazily. If only the tall, handsome man in her kitchen would step a little closer still and maybe lean in for a—

The doorbell rang. She filed her fantasy away for another time and pointed to the back door. "This is your last chance to escape," she teased. "Otherwise, prepare to meet some of the founding families of our town. Or at least the ones I know."

"I don't scare easy. Lead on."

She walked into the living room and saw that several couples had arrived at once. The next few minutes passed in a blur of introductions. Madeline was pleased that no one was overly shocked to find Jonny Blaze in her living room. Or maybe they were like her—secretly stunned, but keeping their reaction to themselves.

She went back to the kitchen to start piling goodies onto platters. There were cookies and brownies and bars of all kinds. Shelby came in and walked to the sink where she washed her hands.

"So, how's it going?" her friend asked.

Madeline smiled. "Fine. Did you have a nice dinner?"

"Sure. Kipling and Destiny are always fun to hang out with. And I adore Starr."

Starr was Destiny's half sister. The teen lived with them.

Shelby dried her hands, then started adding more cookies onto platters.

"Want to talk about it?"

Madeline widened her eyes, as if confused. "Talk about what?"

Shelby put down the brownies and settled her hands on her hips. "Jonny Blaze is standing in your living room. Last I heard, you had a serious crush on him. Serious to the point that you couldn't even look in his direction, and now he's here?"

Madeline grinned. "I know. It's so strange."

"And?"

Madeline finished filling the plate, then faced her friend. "It's all Mayor Marsha's fault."

"Most things are."

She quickly explained about the wedding and how she was now spending time with the action star.

"Are you freaked?" Shelby asked.

Madeline realized Isabel had voiced the same concern. She must have really been acting strange when Jonny was nearby. "At first, but it's getting better. He had dinner here. That was surreal. But my parents took it in stride and I pretended that I was just as calm."

"Has he kissed you?"

The unexpected question caused Madeline to flush. "What? No. We're working together. Besides, I'm, you know, regular. He's Jonny Blaze."

"I'm sure he's just as interested in sex as the next guy."

"Shelby, no." Madeline glanced around to make sure no one was nearby. "It's not like that. He would never want that from me."

"Then he's an idiot. You're great."

Because Shelby was a loyal friend. Madeline knew that she was pretty enough for regular people, but in the sphere that was Jonny's world? Not so much.

"It's okay. I'm getting over my crush and enjoying what I know is very one-sided sparkage. It's nice. My own little fantasy holiday entertainment. I'm also having fun planning the wedding. It's different. I haven't met Ginger yet, but we talked on the phone and she's really nice."

"When he comes to his senses and ravishes you, I want details," Shelby told her. "I'm in a very arid dry spell. I will live vicariously through you."

Madeline pretended to fan herself. "I hope I have something to share."

They both picked up plates of treats and carried them back to the living room.

In the few minutes Madeline had been in the kitchen,

more people had arrived. She saw Jonny talking to a couple of the guys from CDS—or as the locals knew it, the bodyguard school. It was interesting, watching them together. Ford and Angel were both physically powerful and good-looking, but there was something compelling about Jonny. She supposed that was a lot of the reason he was successful in movies. You wanted to watch him.

"Hey."

Madeline turned and saw Consuelo Hendrix standing next to her. "Hi."

"Nice party."

Madeline nodded because she was unable to speak. She knew it was shock at how her friend was dressed, and when Consuelo noticed, there was going to be ugly punishment, but still. She couldn't help staring.

She and Consuelo had been friends for a couple of years. Nearly since the other woman had moved to Fool's Gold. Consuelo had worked for the government, doing things that she never talked about. Despite her petite build, she was tough and dangerous. She didn't do emotion, she moved like a prowling leopard and her idea of relaxation was to go climb a mountain.

She taught all kinds of fighting techniques at the bodyguard school, along with mixed martial arts to people in town. Her everyday wardrobe consisted of cargo pants and boots. In the summer they were worn with a tank top or T-shirt. In the winter, a light sweatshirt.

But tonight she had on a fitted black dress. Simple, really, with a scoop neck, a straight skirt and long sleeves. With it she wore thigh-high leather boots with a serious heel. The church-appropriate dress paired with very naughty boots was pure Consuelo. When placed on her perfect, athletic body, the results were incredible. And intimidating.

"What?" Consuelo demanded, her voice challenging. "You want to say it, so say it."

"You look beautiful."

Consuelo's eyebrows drew together. "Don't make me kill you."

Madeline held out the plate. "Sugar cookie? My mom made them."

Consuelo took one. "Don't think you can distract me from the compliment."

"You do look lovely."

Consuelo groaned. "I knew it was a mistake. I told Kent, but he said that just once he wanted to see me in a dress. So what the hell, right? It's the holidays."

Madeline laughed. "You are incredibly strange."

"I know." Consuelo stepped back and then looked down at herself. "It's not too much?"

"Like I said—you're beautiful. Sexy, too. I'm amazed you made it to the party on time," Madeline murmured. "I'm assuming Kent knows he's a lucky man."

"He does." She glanced around at the people laughing and talking. "Who's that guy? He looks familiar."

Madeline didn't have to turn around. "Jonny Blaze." She waited for the shriek, or at least the semishriek. Consuelo was always controlled.

"Oh, right. I should have recognized him. I like his movies. He gets it right. The fighting." Consuelo rolled her eyes. "You have no idea how many actions scenes are completely screwed up. It makes the movie or TV show impossible to enjoy. Kent says I should be more forgiving."

"Not gonna happen?" Madeline asked with a grin.

"You know it."

"Come on. I'll introduce you."

Madeline walked over to where Jonny was now talking to a couple of guys from Score, a local PR firm owned by former NFL stars. As soon as she approached, Jonny turned to her.

"This is my friend Consuelo," she told him. "She works at CDS."

"The bodyguard school," he said, looking at the other woman. "Jonny Blaze. Nice to meet you." They shook hands. "I met Angel and Ford a few minutes ago. They were talking about you."

Consuelo groaned. "Don't believe them. It's all lies. I like what you did in *Amish Revenge*. That last scene—on the train. It was authentic."

"Thanks. It was all me and I have the bruises to prove it."

Everyone else chuckled, but Consuelo just kept talking. "The fight scene before sucked, though. You didn't have the moves down. You have a trainer, right? He blew it. It's not your fault."

Madeline wanted to sink into the floor and come out on the other side of the planet. Had her friend really said that? Not that she should be surprised. Consuelo spoke her mind and usually followed up her opinions with threats.

She waited for Jonny to change the subject or get upset or maybe even leave. Instead, he nodded. "You're right. We couldn't seem to figure out the flow. I don't suppose you have training with a knife?"

Consuelo grinned. "Are you kidding? I'm all about fighting with a knife."

"For real? Because I'm interested. Do you have a class or something?"

"Not for knife fighting. I don't think Mayor Masha

would approve. But I could show you a few things. Call CDS and set up an appointment."

"I will."

Kent walked over to his wife. "Trying to make me jealous?" He nodded at Jonny. "Kent Hendrix."

They two men shook hands.

"Your wife was talking to me about my knife fights," Jonny explained.

"Of course she was." Kent kissed the top of Consuelo's head. "I can't take you anywhere."

"That's what I keep saying," she complained. "And you keep dragging me places. Why is that?"

Kent laughed.

Several people drifted away, while others joined them. Jonny moved closer to Madeline.

"You know some interesting people," he said.

"Consuelo is in a class by herself. But you're right. We have fascinating residents. It's nice and keeps things fun."

"I hope she meant what she said about teaching me some moves."

"You could hire her as a consultant on your next movie."

Instead of laughing, as she'd expected, he nodded slowly. "That's a good idea. I'll talk to her about it next week. If she's interested, I can—"

He stopped talking and stared over her head. "No way."

She turned to see what had caught his attention. The Strykers had arrived. Three brothers and their wives.

"What?" she asked before all the breath left her body.

Jonny grabbed her hand and pulled her across the room. "I don't believe it," he said.

She couldn't, either. Not the dragging part but the way he was holding her hand. Just as if they were... She wasn't sure what. Friends? Lovers?

His long fingers laced with hers. His palm was warm and his touch...tingled. She didn't know what to think, what to say. Begging him to never let go seemed out of place at this holiday gathering. And she had the oddest impression he had no idea what he was doing.

"Clay," Jonny said, coming to a stop in front of the youngest Stryker brother. "What are you doing here?"

Clay stared for a second, then laughed. "I could ask the same thing. You in Fool's Gold?"

"I bought a place outside of town."

"I have a haycation business. Farm vacations." He drew his wife close. "Honey, this is Jonny Blaze. We've worked together. Jonny, my wife, Charlie."

Sadly, Jonny had to release Madeline's hand to shake

Charlie's. Madeline had known the other woman for years and had, until that moment, liked her a lot.

Jonny grinned at her. "Clay's a great guy. We had a lot of fun on the set."

Clay shrugged. "That was a while ago. We were both younger."

Madeline thought about Clay's former profession. "When you say worked together," she began.

Jonny chuckled. "Clay was my butt double on *Amish Revenge*."

Various scenes flashed in her mind, including the one where Jonny had walked naked through the house. From the front there had been no "below the waist" shots, but from the back, there had been a single, long, slow pan from neck to feet.

"That wasn't you?" she asked, hoping the disappointment didn't show in her voice.

Charlie leaned against her husband. "I can attest that what you saw on the big screen was all Clay." She looked at Jonny. "Didn't have the goods, huh?"

Jonny's good humor didn't fade. "I have the goods," he said easily.

Clay nodded. "He would have been fine on his own. What Jonny won't say is that the first actor hired for the role had insisted on a butt double. When he dropped out and they hired Jonny, he could have canceled the contract, but he didn't. It was a big break for me in the business."

Madeline's head was swirling from too much information. First, that Jonny hadn't been the producers' first choice for the movie that had basically made his career. Second, that even then, he'd been such a nice guy, giving Clay a job. Third, that the man had held her hand.

"Be careful," Charlie told him. "If Eddie and Gladys get ahold of you, you're toast."

With that, the other couple moved away. Jonny turned to Madeline. "I met Gladys, but who's Eddie?"

"They're two older women who have a cable access show," she explained. "One of their most popular segments is a contest where they show pictures of men's butts. You have to guess who the men are and text in your answer."

His dark green eyes widened. "Seriously?"

"You can't make stuff like that up."

"I guess not." He shrugged. "I was expecting bake sales and toy drives. Not butt contests."

"We're a constant surprise."

"Did you mention the toy drive?" Taryn asked as she walked by. "Do you know something? Should I worry?" She paused. "Oh, hello. You're Jonny Blaze. Taryn Crawford. You met my husband earlier. Angel—with the bodyguard school."

"As far as I know, everything is on track for the toy drive," Madeline assured her.

Taryn, ever fashionable in a dark violet dress that matched her eyes, sighed. "We do a toy drive between Thanksgiving and Christmas. Last year I was smart enough to be on vacation. This year, I'm here and feeling the pressure."

"What kind of toys are you looking for?" Jonny asked.

Both women stared at him.

"What kind do you have?" Taryn asked.

Madeline expected him to say something like he was happy to write a check. Instead, he hesitated.

"I have some carved wooden toys. They're a little old-fashioned." He shifted from foot to foot. "There's a lot of extra time on a movie set and it helps to have a hobby. When I was filming *Amish Revenge*, we had a couple of Amish men as consultants. One of them taught me how to do wood carving. I do toys."

Taryn's gaze sharpened. "Like trains and little animals?"

"Something like that."

"We'll take them. Seriously. Kids love to use their imagination. Can I reach you through Madeline?"

He nodded.

"Great. I'll be in touch."

Curiouser and curiouser, Madeline thought as she introduced Jonny to more people. The man was nice and good-looking and he loved his sister and he carved wooden toys. Who could resist that? Even if there hadn't been massive tingles during a simple and not even conscious handholding, she would have been swept away. A regular girl didn't have a chance.

Two hours later, Jonny stood by the front door. "I had a great time. Thanks for inviting me today."

"You're welcome." She wanted to say more, but couldn't think of any words. Not when he was lowering his head in a very deliberate way.

Oh, God! He was going to kiss her. Right in her doorway, with her parents and older brother not ten feet away. Okay. She could do this. She could—

He brushed his mouth against her cheek. "I'll see you soon."

Disappointment chased away any tingles, leaving her grumpy. On the cheek? Like she was ten? What about a little lip action? Some tongue? She wanted tongue.

As she wasn't going to get any, she closed the front door and walked into the kitchen to help with the rest of the cleanup. Her mother already had the dishwasher full again and was pouring in soap.

"That went well," she said as she straightened. "I do enjoy seeing everyone."

"It was great. I can't believe how much everyone ate. They had to have been stuffed from their dinner, but still. It's your amazing recipes, Mom. You do cookie magic."

"You're sweet. No magic. Just lots of sugar." Her mother leaned against the counter. "Jonny was very nice. He fit in well." Her gaze sharpened. "Any lightning strikes? You know how it is in our family. You'll know when you've found the one by the lightning strikes."

Madeline did know, and at nearly twenty-nine, she had never even felt the slightest of buzzes. It was kind of depressing. Not counting Jonny, of course. With him there were zips and zings and, yes, lightning.

"Mom, he's great. But whatever I feel around him isn't real. It's star power. Something about having the biggest head in the village."

Her mother frowned. "What?"

Madeline made a note to talk to Felicia and get clarification on the whole important-in-the-village theory. "Okay, it's not that, but it's because he's famous. I feel like I know him, so when we're together, I'm reacting to that. Not who he is as a person."

"You're judging him on what he does for a living," Loretta pointed out. "How interesting. You wouldn't do that if he didn't have an impressive job."

"This is different."

"If you say so." Her mother hugged her. "Happy Thanksgiving. You're my favorite daughter. Have I mentioned that?"

Madeline laughed and hugged her back. "Once or twice, and I appreciate it every time."

Late Friday morning Jonny was back in town. He'd spent a couple of hours on the internet and had some wedding ideas he wanted to discuss with Madeline. But first he wanted to see the town's transformation from Thanksgiving to Christmas.

According to the festival schedule that had been part of his welcome packet, the town tree lighting was Saturday at six. As of the parade yesterday, Fool's Gold had been turkey central. But by eleven on Friday morning, there wasn't a gourd to be found.

Instead, he saw snowmen and elves and Santas filling store windows. Workers strung lights and the harvest flags were being replaced with celebrations of Christmas, Hanukkah and Kwanzaa. A truck carrying a huge Christmas tree rumbled down Frank Lane.

Since Ginger had graduated high school and headed to college, the holidays hadn't been that big a deal for him. Now he found himself enjoying the anticipation of celebrating the season.

He walked into Brew-haha and waited in line. The cheerful store had already put up a small tree in the corner. There were three different nativities on the shelves and paper snowflakes hanging from the ceiling.

When he reached the front of the line, the woman taking orders smiled at him.

"I heard you have toys for the toy drive," she said. "That's great. We're hoping to fill two trucks this year."

Word traveled fast, he thought. "The toys aren't ready," he said. "They need to be painted."

"That's okay. You have a couple of weeks. Or you can ask for help. We're always happy to step in."

"Thanks." He placed his order, then went to wait.

He shouldn't be surprised that someone who hadn't been at the party last night already knew about his offer. He would guess the sharing had nothing to do with him and everything to do will filling two trucks with toys.

He'd made the right decision to move here, he thought. Maybe the town wasn't what he was used to but he liked it. He felt comfortable. For a second he allowed himself to believe he could have it all. A wife and a few kids. A normal family. Not that it was really possible. He'd seen what the attention did to those outside of the business. How it ripped families apart. Why would he do that to someone he claimed to love?

But as he took his coffee and headed for Paper Moon, he savored the possibilities. The what-ifs. And unexpectedly, the woman he pictured wasn't his usual faceless stand-in. It was a pretty blonde with an easy laugh. One who had bluntly told him that when it came to weddings, she had no idea what she was doing.

He found Madeline wielding an industrial-size clothing steamer. When she saw him, she turned off the machine and grinned.

"Thanks for rescuing me. Rosalind had a sudden rush of shoppers Wednesday afternoon. That generally ends with wrinkled samples. They have to be fluffed back to perfection for the next customer, which means steaming. On the bright side, I'm sure the warm, moist air is good for my skin."

He liked the combination of practicality and optimism. She was, he had to admit, a temptation. Were they on a movie set, with a predetermined time limit and a clear understanding that this wasn't going anywhere, he would be making his move. But they weren't. And Madeline was a forever kind of woman. She deserved a man who understood that. A man who could believe in forever.

She led the way to her office. "What's up?"

"I spent a little time online this morning and found some wedding favors." He pulled a couple of sheets of paper out of his jacket pocket.

"I'm impressed that you know what wedding favors are," she admitted.

"I've been reading up." He shrugged out of his jacket, then pointed to the papers. "There's a company that makes custom cookies. They come individually wrapped and can be in different shapes. Ginger and Oliver can have their initials on the cookies or have them shaped like a wedding cake."

Madeline looked at the pictures he'd downloaded. "They're charming," she said. "I love the little cookies in the shape of a wedding cake. That's perfect. And because they're wrapped, the guests can take them with them."

She pulled out a notepad and wrote down the information. "I was going to email Ginger later. Let me include the links. We should have enough time, but I want to get the order in quickly. Just to be on the safe side."

"I also found a couple of ideas for cakes."

He handed over the two photos. Madeline looked at them both. The first was pretty simple. Just three round layers with a few flowers scattered across the icing. There was a band of color at the bottom of each layer that could be customized.

"I didn't know if Ginger had picked colors yet," he said. "The cake could be made to match the decorations."

"Pretty," Madeline said. "Kind of big but—" She turned to the second cake and her mouth parted. "Seriously?"

"I know it's a little larger."

"A little?"

She turned the paper so he could see the picture. Jonny shrugged.

"It's for my sister."

"It's five layers. It would feed three hundred. The guest list hasn't hit fifty."

"It's a statement cake."

He liked how the individual flowers cascaded down the sides. There was a huge spray of them on the top, and more clustered around the bottom.

"The work is all custom," he said. "Normally you have to reserve about two years in advance, but she had a cancellation and we can get one made in time."

"It's huge," Madeline said. "You know this isn't anything like Ginger's described. It's massive and ornate."

"It's beautiful and Ginger deserves the best."

Madeline stared at him for a second before murmuring, "Okay. I'll send her the link."

"We need an answer by Monday. To reserve the big cake."

"Ginger usually gets back to me really quickly. Once she tells me which one she likes, I'll get it ordered. Along with the cookies."

She paused and looked at him. "You know the specialness of the day is about Ginger and Oliver and having the people they love around them when they say their vows. It's not about the cake."

He got the message, and while he knew Madeline was right, he didn't want to scrimp. "I want her to be happy. I want her to know she's important to me."

"Don't you think she already does?"

"The cake will seal the deal."

"If you say so."

❧ FIVE ❧

Late afternoon on Saturday Jonny was done pretending. He'd spent the day at his house, reading scripts and working out. The usual stuff. But he'd been restless and watching the clock. A little after four he drove to town and found parking, then walked through the growing crowd.

The Christmas tree lighting was at six. Before then there were carolers in the street and a couple of bands. Food carts lined the edge of the park. Lots of local businesses had put up their own trees with different themes. The one by Jo's Bar had pet ornaments that represented several dog breeds, including a dachshund ornament.

Several people he passed called out greetings. He recognized a lot of couples from the party at Madeline's house. All the while he chatted and ate a pretzel, he found himself looking for someone.

She had to be here. It was a family tradition. But try as he might, he couldn't spot Madeline anywhere.

At five-thirty, he'd about given up. Just when he was thinking he might as well head home, a familiar voice called his name. He turned and saw Loretta walking toward him.

"I thought I recognized you," Madeline's mother said, surprising him by hugging him. "Are you here to see the tree lighting?"

"Sure."

She held him close a half second longer than he thought she would. Like a mom. He'd lost his mother when Ginger had been born and his dad hadn't been one to date so there'd never been a woman around to take care of things. While his dad did his best, some things had been lacking.

Loretta released him and smiled. "Then come watch with us. These kinds of things are better when shared."

She linked arms with him and led him toward the right side of the square. There were people everywhere, but she wove through them, guiding him to a destination he hoped included her daughter.

"Joseph and I used to bring Robbie here when he was little," she said. "About the time he turned fourteen, he decided he was too mature to bother with silly traditions.

So we left him home. When we got back, we found him crying in his room. It was the last time he missed the tree lighting." She sighed. "Then we had Maddie and got to start all over with a new little one."

"You were lucky with both your kids," he told her.

"We were. Very lucky. Children are a blessing." She glanced at him. "You don't have any?"

"No. I'm not married."

The smile returned. "These days marriage is more of an afterthought. Not always necessary."

"I'm a traditional guy." He wanted a wife—someone who was a partner. He wanted to be there for someone and to be able to depend on her in return.

"So what's the problem?" Loretta asked, her tone light. "From what I can tell, women find you attractive. You have a job and you can carry on a conversation. They could do worse."

He grinned. "Thanks for the vote of confidence."

"I like to see the best in people. I'm sure you have your flaws."

"I do, but let's not talk about them."

"Which means I'll ask the question again. What's the problem?"

"What I do, who I am, makes it difficult to have a serious relationship. There are outside pressures. The press gets in the way. The fame."

Loretta stopped walking and studied him for a second before glancing around. "Am I missing them?"

The question was asked in a gentle tone, but the words made him feel foolish. "It's different here," he mumbled. "Trust me—it can be intense."

"I'm sure it can. I just wonder…" She stared into his eyes. "Jonny, have you ever been in love?"

"No."

She tucked her arm in the crook of his elbow and moved through the crowd. "You need to give it a try. Falling in love is magical. I remember the day I met Joseph. There was no warning. I was minding my own business when there he was. He smiled and introduced himself and that was it. I felt it."

"Felt what?"

"Lightning. I was struck by lightning. Oh, there are other ways to describe it, but the truth is I knew from that moment he was the one. Fortunately, he felt the same way. We've been together forty-eight years." She smiled. "I won't lie and say there haven't been times I wanted to back the car over him. Living with someone is always a challenge. But there hasn't been a single day that I haven't been grateful to have found him. Joseph has given me a wonderful life and two beautiful children. I want that for you."

"Joseph isn't my type."

She laughed. "See. You're charming. Put that charm to good use and find a girl. Fall in love. Get married. Have children. You'll be amazed at how happy all that makes you."

He wanted to point out that she didn't know him well enough to make that assessment, but he couldn't help thinking she was right. That was exactly what he wanted.

"You make it sound easy," he told her.

She faced him again. "Love is many things, but it's not easy. It requires everything. Whatever you're most afraid to give is exactly what it will demand of you. But it's worth it. That's the secret. It's worth it."

Before he could ask her what she meant, he spotted the woman he'd been looking for. Madeline hurried over.

"Mom, are you being scary? Jonny looks trapped."

"Not trapped," he assured her. "Mesmerized."

"Uh-huh. If only that were true."

"I found Jonny waiting for the tree lighting and told him he should be with friends."

Madeline looked at him. "You don't have to stay with us."

"I want to," he said, telling the truth. "You have a

tradition and I appreciate the opportunity to be a part of that."

He was going to say more, but the music faded and Mayor Marsha stepped up in front of the microphone.

"Welcome, everyone," she began. "This is our sixty-second tree lighting."

As if on cue, snow began to drift down from the sky.

"How does she do that?" Madeline asked. "I swear, the woman knows God personally."

"Maybe they text."

She laughed. The sound was as light and engaging as the Christmas bells he could hear in the distance. Without considering what it meant or any consequences that could follow, he put his arm around her. For a second Madeline didn't move. Then she leaned into him, snuggling close. Jonny liked the feel of her next to him. He liked her family and this town and the fact that it was only a few weeks until Christmas. Because for now, he could fit in, just like everyone else. And sometimes, that was the best gift of all.

"I'm late," Madeline yelled as she raced to the door of Paper Moon.

"You said that five minutes ago, which means you're

really late," Rosalind called after her. "And I mean that in a helpful way."

"You're such a mom."

"Thanks. Have fun."

Madeline wasn't sure *fun* was the word she would describe where she was going, but it wasn't entirely wrong. Helping out at the holidays was expected and this was her thing.

She would have been on time except for an unforeseen shopper that morning. Apparently her theory about no proposals over Thanksgiving hadn't been correct. One young man had popped the question and a new bride-to-be had wanted to try on dresses.

Now Madeline hurried toward city hall. As it was less than two blocks away, she had a good shot of getting to her meeting before it started.

She waited to cross the street. As she stepped off the curb, Jonny came up beside her.

"Hey," he said. "How's it going?"

"Great."

She told herself to act casual. She hadn't seen him since the tree lighting a couple of days before. The fact that he'd put his arm around her for nearly an hour didn't mean anything. This wasn't high school. He'd been keeping her warm, not stating his intentions. She knew because when the tree lighting had ended, he'd said good-night and walked away without a backward glance. Or a kiss. Was it wrong to want a little tongue for the holidays?

He kept up with her as she circled around city hall to head in the front entrance.

"Did your parents fly out this morning?" he asked.

"Yes. They're in the air on their way back to Florida as we speak."

"Sorry to see them go?"

"Always. They're fun to hang with. My mom is totally freaked about the cruise they booked for the holidays. She's worried I'll be all alone on Christmas. I've told her I'll be fine, but I'm not sure she believes me."

"She loves you and wants you to be happy."

True, but slightly strange to hear him saying that.

She stopped in front of the large, three-story building. "Did we have a meeting? I sent off the email to Ginger about the cake and the other things and she hasn't gotten back to me yet. She and Oliver are going to make their decisions in a day or so."

Jonny nodded. "She told me that, too. She should probably start cc-ing us on the emails so she doesn't have to write two." He glanced at city hall. "What's in there?"

She assumed he was asking what she was going to

be doing, rather than requesting an explanation of city government. "I'm on the Live Nativity committee," she told him. "We're finalizing arrangements for the twenty-fourth."

His brows rose. "Live as in…"

"You have no idea."

"Great. Can I come?"

"To talk about the ramifications of having an elephant in the Live Nativity? It's not that interesting."

"It is to me. It'll be fun."

He started up the stairs without waiting for her, which meant she had to hurry to catch up. The man was nothing if not unexpected, she thought, unclear on any possible interest he could have in the committee.

Once they entered the building they went down the hall, then up the stairs to the second floor.

"The meeting room is down here," she said.

"So why are people upset about the elephant?"

"Aside from the fact that there probably wasn't an elephant around when Baby Jesus was born?"

"Yeah, that."

"Because there are other people with unusual pets who think they should be included. Plus, there was a little pushback when we allowed a service dog, namely a toy poodle, to stand in for Baby Jesus. We were supposed to replace her with a doll, but somehow that didn't happen and, well, there were some letters to the editor."

He grinned. "I love this town."

"You didn't have to deal with the letters."

He held open the door and she stepped into the conference room.

There were four long tables pushed together, forming a square. The chairs were on the outside. Madeline saw that Mayor Marsha was nowhere to be seen, which most likely meant the other woman wasn't going to attend. Mayor Marsha was nothing if not prompt. Dr. Galloway, the committee chair, was also absent, but as there was a folder in front the seat she usually occupied, Madeline figured she would be here any second.

Most of the other chairs were occupied by the usual suspects. Everyone looked up when Jonny entered. Madeline realized she had absolutely no explanation for his presence other than "He thought it would be interesting." Fortunately, Jonny was used to dealing with an audience.

He introduced himself and asked if he could sit in on the meeting. The ten women in the room glanced at each other. They all looked confused, but a couple nodded.

Jonny flashed his movie-star smile, then walked over to sit next to Gladys.

"Thanks for your help the other day," he said.

"It was nothing," she told him. "My great-niece, Nancee, has to deal with difficult situations all the time. She's in Washington, DC, and the things that go on in government…" Gladys shook her head. "Especially when you're young and attractive. But Nancee knows what she wants and it's not a one-night stand with a congressional aid or lobbyist."

Madeline took a seat across from Jonny and smiled sweetly. "You wanted to come with me," she murmured.

Eddie sat next to Gladys. She peered around her friend.

"You're attractive," the seventysomething said.

"No," Madeline told her. "Whatever you're thinking, no. You can't, you won't, you shouldn't and no."

Eddie glanced at Madeline. "You used to be such a sweet little girl."

Madeline was undeterred. "I know and that has nothing to do with this."

"What is she thinking?" Jonny asked.

Madeline groaned.

Gladys looked from her friend to Jonny. "You think?" she asked.

"Of course." Eddie leaned toward him. "Gladys and I have a cable access show."

The other women started to smile. Madeline thought briefly about screaming but didn't think that would distract either of the old women. They were nothing if not tenacious.

"You want me to be a guest?" Jonny asked.

"Not all of you," Eddie told him. "We hold a contest every week. Guess That Butt. We show pictures of butts and viewers text in who they think that butt belongs to. It's an honor to be chosen."

Jonny looked at Madeline. "So you weren't kidding."

"I told you, but did you listen? Yes, this is real. But they left out a very significant detail." She stared at the two women. "Do you want to tell him?"

"It's male butts," Gladys offered.

Eddie grinned. "*Naked* male butts. That's very important." Her smile faded. "But come to think of it, I'm not sure you would qualify. Didn't you use Clay Stryker as a butt double in *Amish Revenge*? Why would you do that? Is there a problem?"

The two old women looked at each other, then back at him.

"Something you can't talk about?" Gladys added in a low, concerned voice.

Everyone else at the meeting leaned forward, as if desperate to know. Madeline wanted to bang her head against the table.

"We're here for the Live Nativity," she said, knowing her mother would be proud of her for being mature. "Let's get back to that."

"Dr. Galloway isn't here yet," Eddie pointed out. "We can't start without the committee chair."

Before Madeline could think of a comeback to that, Jonny stood.

"There's nothing wrong with my butt," he told Eddie and Gladys.

"Prove it," Eddie said firmly.

Before Madeline could figure out what was happening, Jonny turned his back on the room, unfastened his jeans and…

"Oh, my," Eddie and Gladys breathed together. The other women sighed collectively.

Madeline had to agree. Jonny's decision to use a butt double had nothing to do with the body part in question. It was perfect. Muscled and just the right size.

"Is it hot in here?" one of the other women asked as she fanned herself.

Madeline had to admit, she was feeling a little heat herself. Jonny pulled up his jeans, fastened them and settled back in his chair.

"Any questions?" he asked.

"We'll sign you right up," Gladys said.

The door opened and Dr. Galloway walked in. The woman walked briskly to her seat.

"Sorry I'm late. Some of my appointments took longer than expected. What did I miss?"

"Nothing at all," Gladys told her. "I'll start. As most of you know, we've had a couple of animal suggestions for the Live Nativity. The two that make the most sense are the fainting goat and the potbellied pig."

"How does a fainting goat make sense?" one woman asked.

"You didn't see the other animals nominated. These two are the right size, clean and socialized."

"But if the goat faints, won't that be a problem?"

Madeline stole a glance at Jonny. He was listening attentively, looking perfectly calm. Not at all as if the man had just *dropped trou* and flashed them. Although there hadn't been any complaints.

Before she could turn away, Jonny looked at her and winked. She had to bite her lower lip to keep from laughing.

The man had style—she would give him that. And a superior butt. That was kind of a nice combination.

Jonny had done some remodeling to the kitchen and family room when he'd bought his ranch. Outside, he'd converted the two big barns into workable space. One was the open area where he would host Ginger's wedding. The other had been divided into a large workout room and a smaller wood shop. The former was a requirement of his job. Staying in shape was critical. Nobody wanted to see a flabby action star. The latter was where he escaped.

He clicked on lights and stepped into the shop. The toys he'd already finished lined several shelves. He ignored the projects still under construction. Carving took time and he was on a deadline.

Jonny counted forty-seven toys. He sorted by type and counted again. The number was still the same. It was way more than he'd expected. Of course, he'd been carving for several years and hadn't done anything with them.

There were trains and trucks, several small dinosaurs, pull toys and even two twelve-inch-tall castles. Everything was sanded and ready to go, except they were unfinished wood.

The easiest thing would be to put on a kid-safe coating, which would work for some, but the rest should be painted different colors. He had the nontoxic acrylics already, but there was a time constraint.

He decided to choose a few color schemes, then figure out a schedule and see how many he could get done for the toy drive. Next year he would start earlier and be able to donate more.

He shrugged out of his jacket and set his cell phone on the table. Thanks to the zealous concern of the local search and rescue program, there was a new cell tower on the edge of his property and excellent coverage all around the house and barns.

He reached for the first toy. It was a simple truck. Stain or paint, he wondered, before leaning back in his chair. Maybe there was someone he could ask. A person with artistic ability and an eye for color.

He immediately thought of Madeline but figured he was already taking advantage of her. After all, she wasn't getting paid for her work on the wedding. A donation to charity didn't actually count as a paycheck.

Thinking about Madeline made him remember her mother and the conversation he'd had with Loretta the evening of the Christmas tree lighting. How she'd talked about falling in love with Joseph and that she'd simply known he was the one.

Jonny had never felt that. Not lightning, not certainty. He'd dated, but there had always been a reason to move on. Excluding family, he would say the only woman he'd loved had been Kristen. But that had been a long time ago. He'd gone into the relationship aware she was dying and when she'd passed...

He shook his head. Knowing the end was coming hadn't made it any easier to deal with. And since then, he'd avoided entanglements of the romantic kind. Some of it had been Ginger. After their dad had died, he'd been busy making sure she finished high school and got settled at college. She was smart, but not all that great out in the world. He'd wanted to look out for her.

Once she'd gotten her feet under her, he'd thought he might find somebody, but by then he'd been famous and having a relationship in Hollywood wasn't easy. He always had to figure out if the woman in question was interested in him as a man or simply wanted to say she'd slept with Jonny Blaze. Once that hurdle had been cleared, there were other problems. The press, trying to be normal. In the end, it was easier to be alone. He'd gotten used to the idea.

That was one of the great things about living in Fool's Gold. He was a part of the town. They didn't care about who he was or what he did for a living. If that meant having his bare ass up on TV, it was a small price to pay.

He liked that he was making friends. Like Madeline. She was a sweet person with a great sense of humor. The fact that every now and then he found himself wanting to see more of her, well, that was something he would deal with. Yes, she tempted him romantically, but he knew the danger of getting involved. Better to stay friends. Simpler for him and safer for her.

His cell phone rang. The programmed ringtone had him smiling before he even picked up.

"Hey, gorgeous," he said.

On the other end of the call, a woman laughed. "You sound like you're in a good mood."

"I am. Loving my new place."

"Isn't it rural up there?"

He laughed. "They got electricity just last week, so it's not too bad."

"Now you're making fun of me."

"Because I can."

Annelise had been his manager since he'd been "discovered" on his first movie. She was smart, driven and always looked out for him. In a business where managers sometimes had an agenda all their own, Annelise was all about integrity.

"You're ignoring my emails," she said, her tone conversational. "Want to tell me why?"

He thought about the laptop in his office in the house. "I haven't checked it in a few days. Sorry. I'll look at them this afternoon. What's up?"

"The same thing that was up last month. You need to make a decision on the *Amish Revenge* sequel." Her voice softened. "Jonny, I thought you were excited about the project. You're getting a producer credit and can have input on the screenplay revisions. Have you changed your mind?"

He considered the question. The script he'd read had been good. Not just sequel good, but well-written enough to stand on its own. *Amish Revenge* was his most successful movie to date and people wanted to see more of his character.

His reluctance had nothing to do with the project and everything to do with how much he was enjoying regular life.

"I'm in," he told her. "I still want to do the project."

"Then we need you to sign the contract. It's ready to go."

"Okay." He glanced at the clock and thought about the four-hundred-plus-mile drive to LA. "I'll be in your office in the morning."

"I'll see you then."

He hung up, then pushed another couple of buttons and waited. A few seconds later Madeline answered her cell.

"Hello?"

"It's Jonny."

"Oh, hi. I don't think you've called me before. That's why I didn't recognize the number."

He'd given her his cell, but she hadn't bothered to program it into her phone. He wasn't sure what that meant, but it was sure typical of Madeline and the town.

"I have to go to LA for a day or so. I wanted you to know, in case you needed something for the wedding."

She was silent for a second. "Okay. I think I'm going to be fine. Ginger's gotten back to me on the invitations and the cake."

He chuckled. "Let me guess. She went for the big one."

"You know she didn't. Although she did love the cookies as favors for the guests. I've ordered those and the cake. We have colors, by the way. Green and gold. They're going to work beautifully with the invitations, and the cookie lady said she could do trim in those colors, no problem."

"You're taking care of the details. Thanks for that."

"I'm happy to help. Are you really just going to be gone for a couple of days?"

He started to ask if she would miss him, but stopped himself. Mostly because he didn't know the answer to the question. It wasn't the kind of question a guy wanted hanging out there in space.

"That's the plan," he told her, realizing he wanted her to miss him. Even better, she could ask to go with him. He knew a great hotel where they could—

Back the truck up, he told himself. No way he was going there. Madeline deserved more than a couple of nights at a Beverly Hills hotel. She was looking for a lightning bolt. And while no guy could promise that, he wasn't going to treat her like one of his temporary women.

"You need to make sure you're back before the hayrides start," she told him. "I know they sound silly, but they are so much fun. They're out at this ranch and— Oh, it's where Priscilla the elephant lives. The one from the parade."

"Is there more than one elephant?"

She laughed. "No. We just have the one."

"And Reno, her pony."

"They are a couple."

"I'll be back and we'll go on a hayride."

"You'll love it," she promised. "There's hot chocolate at the end."

"Of course there is. Sounds fun."

"Great, it's a date. Have fun in LA. Drive safe."

"I will."

"Bye."

She ended the call. He set down his phone and told himself her "it's a date" comment had been meant in fun. It was an expression, not a promise. Which was kind of too bad.

⊰ SIX ⊱

JONNY DID HIS BEST TO follow along as Annelise walked him through the contract. They were nearly done and normally he found the workings of Hollywood interesting. Just not today.

He kept getting distracted by the very tasteful holiday decorations in his manager's office. There was a small tree in the corner, a flower arrangement on her bookshelves.

"You don't decorate the office yourself, do you?" he asked.

She glanced at him. "It's two more pages. Let's get through them and then we can talk about anything you'd like."

"Slave driver."

"Always."

He forced himself to focus on the small print, then when they'd gone over the final page, he pointed at the tree. "Did you do that?"

"No. Caryn takes care of it. Do you need her to find you a decorator for your new house? I thought you had a guy. Won't he do holidays?"

"He does and he has. I was just wondering about the decorations. Did you know that in Fool's Gold they don't decorate for Christmas until after Thanksgiving?"

Annelise, a pretty woman with long dark hair and an easy smile, gazed at him. "How magical."

"Are you being sarcastic, because it's a very nice town."

"I can tell. I can't wait to visit."

"They have festivals. You'd like that."

"I would. I enjoy visiting small towns."

"As long as at the end of the weekend you get to go home?"

"Exactly."

He turned his attention back to the contract, then signed his name on the line. Annelise passed him the other copies and he did the same.

"I'll call them right away and let them know it's a done deal," she told him. "The locations will be nice. I'll have to visit you there, too."

"You're always welcome."

Amish Revenge 2 would be filmed in Pennsylvania, but there was also going to be at least six weeks in the French and Italian Alps. Madeline's parents had talked about wanting to travel more. He wondered if they would enjoy France or Italy. While he would be busy filming, there would be down days when he could show them around.

He shook his head, knowing he wasn't fooling anyone, especially himself. While he liked Loretta and Joseph, the person he would most want to see in Europe would be Madeline.

Caryn, a tall, twentysomething brunette with streaks of purple in her short hair, walked in with coffee. Jonny took one of the mugs.

"You did a nice job with the decorations," he said.

Caryn smiled at him. "Thanks. I have fun playing in Annelise's office. We only do it at Christmas. Now if you could talk her into decorating for every holiday, that would be great."

"Not going to happen," Annelise said cheerfully. "But you can keep asking."

"I will." Caryn took the empty tray with her as she walked toward the door. "How's your shopping coming?"

"Mine is easy," Jonny told her. "I just have Ginger, and this year I'm giving her a wedding." And a honeymoon, but she didn't know about that. He and Oliver were keeping it a secret until just before the big day. As far as she was concerned, they were going to stay in their apartment for a few days before classes started. Instead, the newly married couple would be flying to Hawaii to spend six nights in an oceanfront suite he'd rented for them.

"Lucky you to be done already," Caryn said. "I have brothers and sisters and now a sister-in-law and my parents. Plus the work presents, but those are fun because I'm not spending my own money."

With that, she walked out of the office. Jonny reached for his coffee.

"Work presents? For the office?"

"No, for clients." Annelise looked at him. "All the things we send out on your behalf." He must have continued to look baffled, because she added, "Gifts for your accountant, your lawyer, the assistant you use on shoots. Like that. There's a long list."

He supposed on some level he'd known this was happening, but he'd never much thought about it. "Shouldn't I buy the presents myself?"

"No. It's part of what we do for you. Besides, most years you're off filming. When would you have the time? Don't worry—we only send nice things. You get very lovely thank-you notes."

"What about you? Does Caryn buy your gift, too?"

"I don't need anything. Jonny, what's going on? You're not yourself."

"Then who am I?"

Annelise picked up her coffee and sipped without saying anything.

He sighed. "I don't know. I'm fine. Just thinking about things. In Fool's Gold I'm not famous. I'm just a regular guy. I like that. Regular guys buy their own presents. They don't hire it out."

"You can't walk into a mall somewhere and shop. Besides, regular or not, you don't particularly like shopping. It's a long list. Do you really want to take it on?"

"No." It was just… He would get Annelise something, he decided. A gift he bought himself because he knew she would like it. And because somehow, in that small act, he would be just like everyone else in Fool's Gold.

Madeline studied the petite blonde with big brown eyes. The dress—a princess style with a full skirt, as requested, hung on her. While it was pretty, it wasn't amazing.

"I don't know," Janet said, then wrinkled her nose. "Am I being too picky?"

"No. Did I say no? Because no. It's your wedding gown. Janet, honey, you have to be picky."

Janet was a sweet girl on her first dress-shopping trip. For reasons she hadn't explained to Madeline, she'd come on her own, which was rare. Brides tended to travel in packs. They might hate Mom's fashion sense but they still wanted her along.

Movement caught her attention. She turned toward the mirror in time to see Jonny walking into Paper Moon. She hadn't seen him in three days and, according to the sudden pounding of her heart, that was two days and twenty-three hours too long.

He looked good. Tall and broad shouldered and impossibly handsome. Her chest got tight, her breathing quickened and she was all about the quivers. Being around him felt like aerobics on demand.

Jonny smiled at her but didn't try to approach. She appreciated that he got she was with a client.

Janet glanced at him. "Oh, hi." She looked back at the mirror. "I just don't know."

"Yes, you do," Madeline said gently. She walked behind the other woman and adjusted the clips holding the dress against her body. "This isn't working. The fit is great and you look adorable but it's not the one."

"How can you tell?"

"Because you're not excited or crying. Both are my favorite, but at least one is required." Madeline removed the clips. "We have lots more dresses to try. You still have the other one you picked. If it's okay with you, I'd like a few minutes to go through my back room. I have a couple of gowns I think would be perfect. You up for that?"

Janet nodded. She blinked a few times, as if holding back tears. "Thanks for helping me."

"Are you kidding? I love this part. When you find the right dress, you'll know. You'll feel the magic all the way down to your toes."

Janet laughed. "That's quite the promise."

"I have no worries about delivering."

She helped the other woman off the dais, then followed her back to the dressing room where she unfastened the dozen or so tiny buttons on the back. She pointed to the robe hanging on the back of the door.

"Go ahead and put that on, then get yourself something to drink and maybe a snack. I'm going to find some treasure for you to consider."

Janet turned around and gave her a quick hug. "Thank you."

"My pleasure, and I mean that."

She let herself out of the dressing room, then went back to where Jonny was waiting.

"Hi," she said, hoping she didn't sound breathless. "I have to go look for dresses."

"No problem." He followed her down the hallway.

"How was your trip to LA?" she asked as she stepped into the storage area and flipped on the light.

There were racks and racks of dresses on two levels. A catwalk surrounded the open room and there were more dresses up there.

"Good. I signed the contract for *Amish Revenge 2*."

She headed for the stairs. "Seriously? That's so great."

"You can't tell anyone."

She reached the catwalk, pausing just long enough to look back at him. "Are you sure? Because that *Hollywood Reporter* guy is calling at three."

"Very funny. You didn't try to sell that girl a dress."

"Janet? The dress she had on didn't suit her at all. She has delicate features and is small boned. The dress overwhelmed her. I knew it wasn't the one, but it was the picture in her head."

She walked to the far side of the catwalk, then began sorting through dresses. She knew the exact one she was looking for.

"Got it," she said, and pulled it off the rack. "I've learned you have to just go with their idea. Sometimes it's right and sometimes it isn't. Once they've seen themselves in a mirror, it's a lot easier to get them to try something else."

"What if she doesn't like any of your choices, either?"

"Then she'll find her dress somewhere else." She draped the dress over the railing. "I'm not saying I don't want the sale. Of course I do. But it's more important that she love her dress. There's no point in forcing a dress on her that she's going to hate."

"How do you know which dress is right?"

"I've done this awhile. Sometimes it's an instinct. Sometimes it's just a matter of trying on different styles." She collected a second dress and started for the stairs. Before she got there, Jonny had climbed to the landing and was holding out his arms.

"What are you doing?" she asked.

"Helping you."

It was sweet. Silly, but sweet. She was up and down the stairs a dozen times a day. But she wasn't going to say that to him. Not when they were standing so close.

With him one step down and her on the landing, they were exactly the same height. She could gaze directly into his beautiful green eyes. She could imagine her mouth pressed against his and feel the warmth of it. If she tossed the dresses over the side and threw herself at him, they could be body to body as they kissed.

Of course, he would be surprised by her rushing him and they would probably fall end over end, down the flight of stairs and be seriously injured, but for one brief shining moment...

She held in a laugh and passed him the dresses.

"Thanks."

"Welcome."

She followed him down the stairs. When they reached the main floor, she took the dresses from him and put them on a rolling rack. She added two others and then looked at him.

"I have to get these to Janet."

"Right. I should go."

Neither of them reached for the door.

"I have to buy a Christmas present," he blurted.

"Excuse me?"

"For my manager. I never have. It turns out that I give lots of gifts every year. I'm sure they're appropriate, but it's not me. It's her staff. Mostly her assistant. I've been with Annelise nearly ten years and I've never bought her a gift."

Madeline was having trouble making sense of the words. "Your manager is a woman?"

"Yeah. She's great. She takes care of me. I want to get

her something. Like a thank-you present, but for Christmas. Where should I shop?"

"At a store? There are several in town. Or online." Didn't the man ever go to the mall, like a regular person?

Madeline thought about the chaos Jonny Blaze would cause in a mall. Okay, that was out. "Oh, there's the gift bazaar this weekend. You could go there. Some of the things are silly, but a lot are nice. There's usually some beautiful artwork and jewelry. Clothes, fudge." She paused to have a taste flashback. "The fudge is really good."

"Want to go with me?"

Naked? Could he be naked? Oh, wait. She didn't want that in public. "Sure. I have a morning appointment, but I'm free in the afternoon."

He flashed her a smile. A beautiful, wide, sexy, Jonny Blaze smile. On the big screen it was pretty compelling, but in person, it left her weak at the knees.

"Thanks," he said, and leaned toward her.

One second there was nothing, the next his mouth brushed against hers. The heat was amazing. Breath-stealing. Perfect.

"I'll see you here at noon. We'll grab lunch, then go to the bazaar."

She nodded because the act of speaking would use too

many brain cells and right now they were busy storing the feel of his warm mouth against hers.

"See you Saturday."

With that, he was gone. Still enjoying the tingle aftermath, Madeline wheeled the dresses toward the changing room and wondered if her math skills were good enough for her to calculate exactly how many hours that was going to be.

Jonny wasn't sure what to expect at the Fool's Gold holiday gift bazaar, but the first thing that stumped him was the location.

"I didn't know this town *had* a convention center," he admitted. He parked his SUV, then looked at the concrete-block structure. "It's kind of ugly."

"I know. One of our only eyesores." Madeline unfastened her seat belt. "But it's a great multipurpose building. We have all kinds of events here, especially at the holidays. *The Dance of the Winter King* has gotten so popular that it had to be moved here, and in a couple of weeks we'll have the annual holiday pet adoption here."

"Pet adoption?"

"Just like it sounds."

"Is there anything the town doesn't do for the holidays?"

"Nothing that isn't good. Although last year someone stole all the toys for the toy drive."

Something he couldn't imagine happening in this place. "Let me guess. In forty-eight hours you had everything replaced, and even more toys than before."

"Something like that," she admitted with a smile.

Her eyes were a pretty shade of blue. She wore her hair loose and had on jeans and a sweatshirt with cartoon reindeer on the front.

In the close confines of his SUV, they seemed to be the only two people in the world. He could inhale the scent of her soap, or maybe it was a light perfume, along with the essence of the woman herself. It was a heady combination. One that made him think that if he were someone else, he would haul her close and kiss her until they were both mindless.

The wanting felt good, he thought. It had been a long time since he'd allowed himself to relax enough to get there. Although he hadn't consciously been easing his guard, there was just something about being around her. She was easy to talk to. Easy to be with. Comfortable, in a way. But sexy. Talk about a combination that was difficult to ignore.

"Ready to be amazed?" she asked.

He was—in every way possible. Even though he knew

she was talking about the gift bazaar and all the crazy Fool's Gold-ness that went with it, he allowed himself to get lost in the possibility, if just for that moment. Knowing there would be hell to pay later, he leaned in and kissed her.

Her mouth was soft and warm. She had on a lip gloss that tasted of peppermint. The SUV console kept them from getting too close, so he couldn't do much more than put his hand on her side and move his mouth against hers.

She yielded. There was no other word to describe her acquiescence as she leaned into him and rested her fingers on his shoulder. Being in a car, the careful way they weren't going for it, reminded him of high school. Back when he'd been like everyone else and life's problems were easily defined.

Wanting filled him, heating him before, predictably, heading south. He wanted to deepen the kiss. He wanted a whole lot more than kissing. Even as his body screamed for him to make his move, his brain reminded him that he liked Madeline. Liked her a lot. So keeping her safe was his first priority.

He drew back.

Her eyes were closed, her cheeks flushed. Then she drew in a breath and looked at him.

"Okay," she murmured. "That was interesting."

He laughed. "Interesting?"

"Unexpected."

"I was hoping for something more."

"Like delicious?"

It was as if someone had kicked him in the gut. All his air rushed out and he was left gasping. Desire exploded and he felt his control being stretched.

He swore silently. He had no one to blame but himself, he thought. He'd asked for it.

"Delicious works," he said, his voice husky. He touched her cheek. "You have no idea how it works."

She studied him. "But? There's a *but* coming. You have *but* face." She looked away, then back at him. "You know what I mean."

"I do. And yes, there's a but. Being with me is difficult. It's the whole public-figure thing. The press can be a problem. I'm not a good bet."

He thought she might say something, push back. Voice an opinion. But she didn't. Instead, she raised her hand, then let it fall back onto her lap.

"So this never happened?" she asked.

"No."

"And you won't do it again?"

"Are you asking me to promise?"

She looked at him for a long time. "You think this is all about you being Jonny Blaze the actor, but you're wrong. Maybe it was at first, but now that I've gotten to know you, it's not."

She opened her car door. "We need to get inside before someone else buys all the good stuff."

With that, she slid out of the SUV.

He followed her, aware that she hadn't answered his question, but still pleased with what she'd said. Because of who she was, he believed her. It was nice to be liked for himself, even if the kissing issue hadn't been resolved.

They walked into the front of the convention center. Tall, seasonally dressed plastic nutcrackers stood guard by the doors. A pleasant woman gave them a map, showing the location of the different booths, and wished them happy shopping.

When they walked inside, Jonny was hit by the volume of noise. There were Christmas carols playing over the speakers and thousands of people talking in a space not designed to dissipate sound in a way that made sense.

Visually, there was just as much going on. Long rows of booths filled the giant room. Hanging banners directed shoppers to different areas. Jewelry, toys and clothes were clearly marked, as were the food areas, holiday decorations and kitchen gadgets.

He considered himself more enlightened than the average male, but even he was overwhelmed by the shopping possibilities. How on earth was he supposed to find a present for Annelise in all this?

Madeline stepped in front of him. Her blue eyes crinkled with amusement as she put her hands on his upper arms and smiled.

"Breathe," she told him firmly. "In and out. No matter how it feels, you will not turn into a woman simply by being here."

"You swear?"

"Yes. Now, we're shopping for your manager, right?"

He nodded.

"Anyone else?"

Friends? Relatives? He'd already taken care of his sister and her husband-to-be. Gifts for Oliver's family had been handled by Caryn. Jonny had seen their names on the list. So there wasn't anyone else.

Except maybe Madeline. He wanted to get her something for helping him with the wedding. Something more personal than the large donation he was going to make. But he wouldn't be buying that here. He would take his time and figure out what it should be.

"Just Annelise," he said.

"Okay. I'm hoping to get a few things for my family," she told him. "If I see something cool for one of my friends, that would be great, but isn't necessary. I already have presents for them. Any thoughts on what you want to get Annelise?"

He thought about the woman who had guided his career for the past decade. "Something personal. For her. Not her office. Something pretty."

"That helps a lot. Clothes are going to be difficult. She won't be able to return them. We'll head toward the jewelry section. I'll bet you can find something there."

He nodded and scanned the row of booths. The jewelry was all the way in the back. "Don't forget the fudge. You said you wanted fudge."

She laughed. "Thanks for remembering. It's my favorite part of the bazaar."

"Then we should get it first." He pointed to the banner above the food section. "It's that way."

They started down an aisle. Within three steps, two groups of women had walked between them. Madeline turned to look for him, just as he came up behind her.

"This could be dangerous," he said with a grin, then took her hand. She laced her fingers with his.

For a second, they looked at each other. He wasn't sure what she was thinking, but his brain settled on several versions of *This is nice.*

They continued walking. Madeline pulled him toward a booth.

"Look," she said, pointing at miniature teddy bears dressed in festive clothes. There were Santa bears and elf bears, bears in pajamas and in scuba gear. She picked up two small bears dressed as a bride and groom.

"Supercute for the table," she told him. "They can be right by where Ginger and Oliver will sit."

The bears weren't his style, but they did remind him of his sister. She had a streak of whimsy every now and then.

"We'll take them," he said, and reached for his wallet.

They made it another ten feet before Madeline pulled him toward another booth. This one sold nutcrackers of all kinds. Madeline settled on one made out of pewter.

"It's a family thing," she told him as she tucked her purchase into the large tote bag she'd brought with her. "I'll send it to Robbie. He and Jasmine collect them."

"Did your mom bring you here every year?" he asked.

She nodded. "It was a big day for us. We'd do a lot of our Christmas shopping. It's where my fudge habit comes from."

They headed in the direction of the food.

"Did your mom always bake?" he asked.

"Every year. It was great. I learned how to make everything, and even when I was a horrible, moody thirteen-year-old, I helped." She smiled at the memory. "When I was little, there were tons of presents. Some from my parents, but most from Santa. As I got older, we shifted to the 'big' gift with several smaller ones."

"Were you crushed about Santa?"

"I heard it from some kids, and while I didn't want to let go, it made sense. What about your Christmases?"

"They were quiet. Just the three of us." His dad had been busy working to keep food on the table. While there had been gifts, they'd been modest. As for Santa, he couldn't remember ever believing.

"You were lucky to grow up here," he said.

"I know. I don't get why people want to move away. I love it."

"When you find Mr. Right, you'll settle here?" he asked.

"I hope so. On both accounts."

"Ever come close?"

"To finding Mr. Right?" She wrinkled her nose. "No. I've never felt the lightning strike my parents talk about. There was a guy in college. Ted. It was serious and then it fell apart. Unfortunately, he's stayed in touch. He and his wife visit every year and it's a nightmare. I swear, the only reason they come here is to rub my face in my singleness. Oh, look. The fudge booth. I'm already feeling the sugar rush."

There was a short line. When they reached the front, Madeline ordered a half pound of three different flavors.

"I'm so going to have to freeze most of this," she murmured as she reached for her wallet. "Or I'll weigh four hundred pounds by New Year's."

"Let me," he said, passing over a couple of bills.

The girl manning the booth took his money. As she started to turn toward the cash register, she swung back. Her eyes widened and her mouth fell open.

"Oh, my God!" she shrieked. "You're… You're…"

He knew what was coming next. She would scream his name and everyone around them would turn and stare. Then people would move close. A few would ask questions while others wanted autographs. The crowd would get bigger and he would have to leave.

Why hadn't he grabbed a baseball cap on his way out? It wasn't the perfect disguise, but it helped. Honest to God, he'd totally forgotten he might cause a problem. Because usually in Fool's Gold, he didn't.

Madeline stepped in front of him and laughed. "He looks like a young Matthew McConaughey, right? We get that all the time. It's really fun. We have a jar where we put five dollars every time it happens." She glanced at him. "Looks like we're that much closer to our trip to New York, honey. Isn't it great?"

The girl stared at Madeline as if she were insane, but when she looked back at him, she was less confident.

"Matthew McConaughey? I was going to say Jonny Blaze."

Madeline frowned. "Seriously?" She turned to Jonny. "Wow, I don't see it. Well, darn. If you're saying Jonny Blaze, I guess we don't get the five dollars in the jar, after all. Unless we include all celebrities. What do you think?"

The girl handed him his change and Madeline the bag of fudge. "Have a nice day," she said pointedly, and looked past them to the customers still in line.

He grabbed Madeline's hand and pulled her away.

"She dismissed us," Madeline said. "I'm shocked. How could she not have an opinion on our New York travel jar?"

He pulled her to the side of the aisle. "Thank you."

"You're welcome. A little misdirection never hurt anyone. I learned it from my brother. Just one of the things he taught me when he came home on vacation."

Jonny put his arm around her. He wanted to do more but there were too many people around.

"He was a good older brother," he said, mostly to distract himself.

"He was. And thankfully gone when I started dating. Otherwise, he would have terrified any date I had. Were you like that with Ginger?"

"I didn't have to be. She didn't date much in high school, and by the time she got to college, she was sensible about guys. I met a few when I visited her in San Francisco and I liked them all."

"What's Oliver like?"

"Nerdy, but in a good way. Crazy about her." He smiled. "He came to ask my permission to propose to Ginger. The poor kid was trembling and sweating. I felt sorry for him, but I made him work for it. They're going to be good together."

"She'll be here in a couple of days. I'm excited to meet her."

He was looking forward to it, as well. He wanted to know what his sister thought of Madeline.

"I'm going to grill her about your romantic past," she teased.

"You can read all about it online."

"I don't think so. Those would be the public relationships. I'm guessing there are some others that no one knows about." She turned to him. "I was kidding. You know that, right? I would never ask Ginger about your love life."

"You didn't even tell your business partner you were helping me," he reminded her. "I know you're joking."

They walked through the crowd to the booths with jewelry displays. Madeline pointed. "Jenel's Gems is a store in town. She has beautiful pieces. You'll want to look at her things for sure."

As they made their way to that display, he spotted a necklace of enamel daisies. The piece was large and gaudy and yet there was something about it.

"For Annelise?" Madeline asked.

"No. I—" He touched the necklace. "I knew a girl who loved daisies." He lowered his arm. "You're right. The significant relationships aren't online. When I was in high school I had a thing for this girl. Kristen. She was beautiful, but aloof. For a year I tried to get close and she wouldn't have anything to do with me."

"What changed her mind?"

"I don't know. Over the summer between our junior and senior year, I kept going by her house. One day she invited me in. She sat me down and told me she had cancer. Something with her blood."

He knew the medical terms and the details, but they wouldn't mean anything to Madeline. He remembered how dispassionate Kristen had been as she'd spoken. As if she were talking about someone else.

Madeline stared at him. "She was sick?"

"She was dying. She told me she only had a few months left and I wouldn't be able to handle it. So there wasn't going to be a relationship ever and I should leave."

He remembered the shock. How he'd been unable to process the information.

"I went back the next day and the next. She finally agreed to see me. We started dating. We had a year. I was there when she died."

He remembered everything about those last weeks, that last day. How her parents had cried, how he'd held her hand and heard her take her last breath. He'd been devastated. Knowing what was going to happen and having it happen weren't the same thing.

Madeline squeezed his hand. "I'm sorry. You've had a lot of loss in your life."

"No more than most. Things happen."

He thought she might say more, but instead she turned to the display and picked up a pair of earrings. There was a knot of gold with a drop pearl.

"Would Annelise like something like this?" she asked.

A graceful shift in subject. He recognized the ploy and was grateful. Once again Madeline had stepped in to save him. He was beginning to think that wasn't just about him. That it was simply a part of who she was.

The man who generated that lightning strike she was waiting for sure was a lucky guy.

·❈ SEVEN ❈·

TWO DAYS LATER, MADELINE'S HEAD was still spinning. Her afternoon with Jonny had been like a roller-coaster ride. Just as soon as she caught her breath, they'd headed around another curve at sixty miles an hour.

The kiss had been wild enough. Just being close to him was enough to send her up in flames, but when he kissed her… She totally lost it. The man was sexy. But it wasn't just because of how he looked—there was how he made her feel. All girlie and safe. When she was around him, she could be herself. Not that she couldn't be around other people. It was just… *Inexplicable*, she thought. That described her feelings exactly.

She'd seen the panic in his eyes when the fudge girl had recognized him. Madeline had jumped in because she hadn't known what else to do. She'd liked that she'd been able to be a distraction, but the taste of what his other life was like had also been a revelation. Then hearing about his first girlfriend and watching how much time and effort he'd put into buying a gift for his manager. Both had surprised her.

The more she knew, the more she liked him. But liking was dangerous and she seriously had to stop it immediately. Not that he was pursuing her. He'd made it clear that as far as he was concerned, it could never work between them.

To be honest, she didn't know what she wanted. Mostly because she already had plenty on her plate and getting her heart broken would be a time suck she didn't want to have to deal with.

She glanced at the clock. Ginger was due any second. She was curious about Jonny's sister. Ginger was sweet in email and on the phone and Madeline was sure they would get along.

At exactly eleven, a petite curly haired brunette walked into Paper Moon. She was small boned, pretty and wearing glasses. She had on jeans and a sweatshirt and carried a simple navy backpack. Clipped to the zipper pull was a small gold star.

"Madeline? I'm Ginger." Her voice was soft, her smile tentative. "Thanks for taking the time to see me today. I know you're busy."

Madeline shook her head. "You're the one who drove

all this way. Thank you for making the time. I know you're overwhelmed with school. Jonny swears you're going to save the world, or cure diseases or something. He's never clear but it's always good."

Ginger laughed. "He's very supportive, even though he has no idea what I'm studying. Which is okay. It's kind of technical and not that interesting to other people."

"Come on back to my office. I have lots to show you."

Madeline led the way. She'd already gone by Plants for the Planet to pick up a few sample flowers. She had pictures for the bouquets, along with some ideas for table decorations. She also wanted Ginger to see the card stock for the invitations. Even though they were already ordered, if Ginger hated them, then they would have to start over.

She pulled her chair around to the front of her desk, so she and Ginger could sit next to each other.

"Here's the card stock," she said. "You've approved the design. If you want different paper, we still have time to make a change."

The other woman fingered the heavy paper. "This is nice. It's just an invitation. As long as everything is spelled right, I'm good."

"I think we're going to get along just fine."

Ginger grinned. "Oliver and I don't want anything

fancy. We're not those kind of people. We're focused on our work and finishing school. But we do want to be married."

Ginger and Jonny shared eye color. Madeline thought she saw similarities in their smiles, although their builds were completely different.

"Here are some flower choices. We'll source locally. I've talked to the owner and she can pretty much get anything. Given the number of people and the space, I'm thinking a U-shaped setup for the tables, so low arrangements would work best. That way everyone can see everything. I was thinking white roses as the base. See the shades of green in these small flowers?"

Madeline showed her the pictures of several different styles of arrangements.

"These variations would be pretty together. We want unscented flowers, or as close to unscented as possible." Madeline flipped to another design. "My friend Dellina is a professional party planner and she says nothing spoils an event faster than stinky flowers."

"Nothing stinky," Ginger agreed. "I think these are all pretty. I like roses."

Madeline stood and picked up a few more samples she'd collected. "Okay. If we stick with white roses as the predominant flower, plus these little green ones mixed in, I was thinking we could use these to hold them."

She set a rectangular barn-wood planter on her desk. "Plants for the Planet has about ten of these, which is more than we need. The rustic feel fits in great with the barn setting and I think will be a nice contrast for the formality of the roses. They also have dozens and dozens of little glass candle holders."

Madeline showed her one. "We can wrap a pretty gold ribbon around them to make them festive and have them blend in with the color scheme. The candles that fit in here last between ten and fifteen hours. That means we can have them lit before everyone arrives. It will be really beautiful."

Ginger sighed. "I love your ideas. The planters, the candles. They're perfect."

"Good." Madeline made some notes. "Now about the cake."

Ginger rolled her eyes. "I saw the one you suggested and the one my brother found. Seriously? This isn't a White House wedding. What was he thinking?" She held up her hand. "Never mind. Don't try to answer that. I like the smaller one you suggested. I love the idea of the white frosting with the green ribbon."

"I'm glad. I've spoken with the cake person and she

can put little gold leaves around the base, to tie in the colors." She made more notes, then put down her pen. "Ready to try on dresses?"

"Yes, but I'm nervous, too."

"That's perfectly normal. Come on. I have a dressing room all set for you." Madeline eyed her. "You're a size six?"

"How did you know?"

"It's my job. Samples are usually a ten. I have a few that are smaller. Based on our emails, I've put some aside for you to try on. I also have a couple I can order from other stores. Let's try on a half dozen or so and narrow down the style."

Ginger stood. Her brows drew together. "I don't understand. I'm not getting my dress today?"

"I don't know. You might. If not, we can do one more try-on session closer to the wedding. I've already reserved my best seamstress for the two days before Christmas. She can work miracles." Madeline smiled at her. "Even though we're getting this done quickly, you have to love your dress. It's a rule."

"If you insist."

"I do."

Madeline led the way toward the dressing room. "The gowns I've pulled are relatively simple. You're petite and that means we have to be careful with proportions. You don't want the dress to overwhelm you. You're wearing *it*, not the other way around. You said you didn't want a bunch of fussy details, so I avoided those."

She opened the door and waved Ginger inside. "There are three dresses. Call me when you're in the first one and I'll come help with the buttons and zippers. Don't worry about the fit. We'll clip it so you can see what the dress will look like when it's altered to fit you."

An hour later they were in agreement that a modified A-line was the way to go. Ginger studied herself in the half circle of mirrors in the main part of the store.

"I like it," she said, her tone doubtful.

Madeline stood behind her and adjusted a couple of the clips. The fit was okay, but the dress wasn't the one, she thought.

"It's too simple," Madeline said. "There's a difference between elegant and plain and we've crossed that line."

Ginger nodded slowly. "You're right. I want something." She pointed at the neckline. "Lace or beading."

"I agree. I have a couple of ideas. I'll email you pictures and then get at least three dresses in right before Christmas."

"Should we hold this one as a backup?"

"Absolutely." Madeline knew they would find the right

dress for Ginger, but also didn't want the other woman worrying. If having a backup dress allowed her to let it go for the next couple of weeks, then they would have a backup dress.

After Ginger changed back into the street clothes, she walked out of the dressing room.

"You've been so great," she said. "Thank you for all your help. There's no way I could do my work and plan a wedding."

"I'm happy to do it," Madeline told her. "I'm having fun and learning a lot about planning a wedding. There are a lot of details. Your brother always has interesting ideas."

She'd meant the comment to be teasing, but instead of smiling, Ginger shifted her backpack from one shoulder to the other.

"We should probably talk about him," she said with a sigh.

Madeline felt herself flush. Oh, no. Was it that obvious that she had a thing for him? Was Ginger going to warn her off? Talk about humiliating.

"My brother is going to be a problem," Ginger said softly. "It's already started. That huge flower cake? What was he thinking? I've told him I want a small, simple wedding. He says he gets it and then he tries to buy a cake like that."

Madeline nodded without actually getting the problem. "Too much involvement?" she asked.

"Trying to show me how much he cares." Ginger pressed her lips together. "You two are friends, aren't you?"

"I think so. He's nice." She didn't know what else to say. Mentioning the tingles wasn't appropriate. Talk about the weirdest conversation ever.

Ginger smiled. "Not many people would describe him as nice, but you're right. He is. He loves me. A lot. Which shouldn't be a problem. Only he wants me to know he loves me and, for Jonny, that means showing, not telling."

"I don't understand."

"He can't say the words. I think it's all the loss he's had in his life."

"Like Kristen?" she said before she could stop herself.

Ginger's green eyes widened. "He told you about her?"

"He, ah, mentioned what happened."

"Then you can see the problem. First our mom, then Kristen, then my dad. Nearly everyone Jonny's ever loved has died. He doesn't want to risk pain again. I can't blame him, but I'm his sister. He's stuck with me. So he doesn't tell me he loves me, he shows me. When I first went to college, he tried to decorate my dorm room. He crammed in so much stuff I couldn't move. He's going to try to do the same with the wedding."

Madeline thought about the giant cake, the extra courses he'd wanted for the dinner and the ice sculptures. "I see what you mean. You want me to keep things in check."

"If you can. I'm not sure it's possible."

"Have you talked to him about this?"

"Dozens of times. He says he gets it, then goes right out and does exactly what he wants. Any help you can give would be really appreciated. Oliver and I want a simple, low-key wedding. I know there are couples who spend years planning the perfect wedding. Oliver and I are more interested in *being* married than *getting* married."

"I understand completely. I'll talk to your brother. If that doesn't work, I'll make sure he doesn't fly in the Vienna Boys' Choir."

Ginger winced. "Please don't mention them to him. I'm sure he would do exactly that."

"It would make for a great story."

Ginger smiled. "We'll have pictures. That's enough."

Madeline hung up the phone and knew that her until-then perfectly wonderful day had been ruined and she had no one to blame but herself. She'd been stupid. Sure there were other words, but that was the truth of it. Dumb her.

She couldn't say why she'd done it, either. The second she'd looked at her cell phone and seen the 509 area code, she'd known. But she'd taken the call, anyway.

"I have to stop," she said aloud as she paced back and forth in her office. "I have to say no. Of course, if I refuse, he wins. If I don't take the call, he wins. And when we go out to dinner, he wins."

"Sounds like you've got a problem."

She spun toward the door and saw Jonny standing just inside her office. He was wearing a leather jacket, jeans and boots. He looked good. Manly. Handsome. Sexy. All things that should have taken her mind off her troubles, but Ted was bigger than all of that. Which was pretty much the worst thing yet.

"You have no idea. But I'll deal. How are things?"

In the world of snappy comebacks and distractions "How are things" wasn't great, but it was the best she could come up with under pressure.

"Fine," he said, walking toward her. "What's wrong?"

"Nothing."

"Something."

She faked a smile. "Nothing I can't handle."

He stopped in front of her and did nothing. He just stood there, as if he had all the time in the world.

"Seriously, I'm fine."

One dark eyebrow rose.

She caved like the weak link she was. "It's Ted. The ex-boyfriend who always comes to town with his beautiful wife."

"The one you told me about?"

She nodded miserably. "Yes. The one who loves to reenact that scene from *Bridget Jones's Diary*." She lowered her voice and tried for a British accent. "So, Bridge, what's it like being perpetually single?" She huffed out air. "It's awful and somehow I agreed to dinner." She squared her shoulders and faked another smile. "It's fine. One night, right? I'm sure being with him and Marigold builds character."

"His wife's name is Marigold?"

"Uh-huh. She used to be a model."

"Runway?"

"Catalog, but still. They talk about it and then ask about my 'retail job.'" She made air quotes. "That's what they call me working here. My retail job. I'm fine with that. I love what I do and I won't apologize for it."

"You shouldn't. You make brides happy. Ted does

weather, so he's wrong sixty percent of the time. How often are you wrong?"

The question made her smile. "A lot less than sixty percent."

"So you win."

If only it were that simple. Despite the dread knotting in her stomach, she didn't want to be whiny. "That's how I need to look at it. Thanks."

"You're welcome." He studied her for a second. "I'll be your date."

She blinked, sure she'd misunderstood. "Excuse me?"

"For the dinner. I'll be your date." One shoulder rose, then fell. "I'm a good date. Not just because you get to bring Jonny Blaze, but because Ted needs to be taken down a peg and I'm the man to do it."

"I, ah, I'm not sure that's a good idea."

"Which part of it?"

The part where she got to walk in with a famous movie star as her date? Or watching said date take down Ted? "It's a little calculated."

"And his invitation isn't? Does it occur to you that Ted and Marigold come here for a reason? One of them needs to show you they're still together and happy. Maybe Ted thinks of you as the one who got away and Marigold wants to be sure you know they're still blissfully happy.

Maybe Ted has a secret thing for you. Maybe they're just jerks. Regardless, there's an agenda. If they get to have one, you should, too."

Madeline felt her mouth drop open. She had never once considered that it was kind of strange her ex-boyfriend visited her every year.

"Wow," she murmured. "You're good."

"Thanks."

"That was really insightful."

One corner of his mouth turned up. "You don't have to sound so surprised."

"Sorry. It's just, you're a guy, plus what Ginger said about—" She slapped her hand over her mouth.

Crap. Double crap. Why had she said that? Now she was going to have backtrack, and with Jonny staring at her expectantly, she didn't know how that was going to happen. It wasn't as if she could think of something else on the spot.

"What did Ginger say?"

"Nothing."

"Madeline, tell me."

She dropped her hand. "You're going to get mad. She loves you and thinks you're great."

His expression was unreadable. That whole actor thing, she thought glumly. Talk about an unfair advantage.

"Do you want coffee? We could get a coffee."

He waited.

"Fine. She said that because of all the loss you've had in your life, you're worried about admitting you care about anyone. That you never tell her you love her. You won't say the words. But you need her to know, so you show it. Sometimes that's great, but sometimes it gets out of hand. Like with the giant wedding cake."

Madeline bit her lower lip and wondered how deep she was digging the hole.

"She knows you love her, Jonny. She doesn't need you to prove that. She's worried the wedding is going to turn into something she doesn't want."

"Did she say that?"

Madeline nodded.

"And ask you to keep me in line?"

"Not in those exact words, but yes."

"Good to know."

With that, he turned and walked away.

Madeline thought about going after him, but there wasn't much else she could say. She'd told him the truth. What he did with it was up to him.

Which was the mature response. The less grown-up part of her pouted at the realization that there was no way Jonny was going to be her date now.

Jonny walked out of Paper Moon with no particular destination in mind. All he knew was he had to get away from the soft, caring worry he saw in Madeline's blue eyes.

She felt bad for him. Him! He was Jonny Blaze. How was that possible? Only she'd been the one delivering the character assessment from his sister. An assessment Ginger hadn't bothered to deliver herself.

He turned left onto Fifth Street, then walked up to Mickey Lane and turned right. The neighborhood was unfamiliar, but solidly residential. Good. He was less likely to run into anyone he knew here.

He looked at the houses lining the street. They were decorated for the holidays with everything from traditional snowmen and Santas to a cement lawn ornament dressed in a Christmas outfit.

Talk about a town that did it up right, he thought. Only they hadn't been talking about the town. Madeline had been talking about him.

He wanted to protest that his sister should have come to him. That she didn't need to be discussing his issues with anyone else. The problem was Ginger had tried many times and he'd refused to listen. Like when she'd turned eighteen and he'd taken her to Europe. Not that uncommon, only he'd arranged for private viewings in several museums and then had flown in three of her closest friends for a girls' weekend in Paris. That might have been a little over the top. Or when he'd rented out the downtown Seattle Nordstrom store for her twenty-first birthday, giving her and her friends free run of the place with the ability to purchase anything they wanted.

While Ginger had appreciated the gesture, she'd patiently explained that a dinner out with him would have been enough. That she knew he loved her and he didn't have to always be showing it. That he could simply tell her instead.

Only he couldn't. He remembered the last time he'd told Kristen he loved her. She'd been fading fast and he hadn't been willing to let her go.

"I love you. If you love me back, you won't die."

"It doesn't work that way." Kristen had smiled then. "I'll love you for the rest of my life. I promise."

A macabre joke—one someone facing death should be allowed. But it had cut him.

He remembered his last conversation with his dad. He and his father had talked about the usual stuff as his father was driving to work and Jonny was getting ready to go to classes at college. They'd ended things as they always had.

"I love you, Dad. I'll call you over the weekend. Have a good day."

"You, too, son."

Two hours later, his father had dropped dead of a heart attack.

Saying you loved someone put everything at risk, he thought. He'd learned that lesson well. While intellectually he knew the words weren't a death sentence, in his gut he wasn't willing to take a chance. So he showed Ginger and sometimes that showing got out of hand. Was that so bad?

He came to a stop on Forest Highway and took a second to figure out where he was in relation to where he'd left his SUV, then he made a right and circled back toward town.

Maybe he should back off a little on the wedding, he thought. The cake had been too big and Ginger was clear on what she wanted. Madeline had a good handle on things. He would trust her, he told himself.

A small import pulled up next to him and the passenger window rolled down. He walked over and saw Mayor Marsha behind the wheel.

"Mr. Blaze," she said cheerfully. "Just the man I was looking for. Do you have a moment?"

"Sure."

"Excellent."

She motioned for him to get in. He did and fastened his seat belt. She started driving.

"Every year we have a Christmas Eve performance called *The Dance of the Winter King*. It's a ballet performed by students here in town. The story is very meaningful and it's all very lovely, as you can imagine."

Kids doing ballet? "I can," he said, doing his best to keep the irony out of his voice.

"There is a narration that goes along with the dance. Usually Morgan does it but he and his family are going to be traveling for the holidays."

Jonny nodded slowly. Mayor Marsha wanted him to narrate the dance. He could do that, he thought. It would be fun. And having his name would be a big—

"I was wondering if you happen to know James Earl Jones," the mayor continued. "He has a wonderful speaking voice and it would be very exciting if we could get him to come to Fool's Gold for the performance."

Jonny stared at her. "James Earl Jones?"

"Yes. Do you know him?"

"Not personally, but I can ask my agent."

"That would be lovely. Thank you."

She pulled up next to his SUV and wished him a good

day. Jonny got out and stared after her. Then he started to laugh.

He'd wanted to be just like everyone else, he reminded himself. He had to remember to be careful what he wished for because it sure as hell had happened.

❧ EIGHT ❧

MADELINE SORTED THROUGH THE VEILS. They were a tangle of lace and tulle, the result of three unexpected brides freaking out about accessories on the same day. Two had placed special orders, one had left in tears.

She rubbed her forehead, hoping the beginnings of a headache would fade rather than grow. Worse, she had to deal with Ted and Marigold that very evening. Because it was just one of those kinds of days.

The front door opened. Rosalind had escaped to the back, leaving Madeline to gather herself and smile sweetly at the—

Only instead of a hysterical bride, Jonny walked in the store. She hadn't seen him since the previous day and she wasn't sure if he would be back. But here he was, striding toward her, looking as sexy as ever.

She let the tingles wash over her. They were a welcome relief from bride stress. When he stopped in front of her, she thought longingly of a kiss. Because a little tongue would go a long way to setting her day to rights.

"I'm still in," he told her. "For the date with Ted. If you're interested."

In having him protect her from Ted and Marigold? In spending an evening with him as his pretend date?

"Yes. I'm interested."

"Good. I'll pick you up at six?"

"Perfect."

"Where should I pick you up?"

"Here. I have to work until we close, then I'll get changed."

"See you then."

Madeline smiled as she realized not only was she going on a date with Jonny Blaze, but that her headache had miraculously faded. Funny how that had happened.

"Don't make me get shrill," Isabel said firmly. "Trust me, with the pregnancy hormones I'm experiencing, shrill is just a heartbeat away."

Madeline studied the beautiful dress her business partner held. It was midnight blue, with a plunging neckline and ruching in all the right places. She'd already tried it on, had spent three days lusting after it, and then had carefully put it back on the rack. The dress was stunning and way too expensive. Her money would be better spent saving to buy another share of Paper Moon.

Now Isabel held out the dress. "I'm serious."

Because her friend was offering it to her for the evening. On a sort of borrow and return program.

"I'm going to mark it down in the morning, anyway," Isabel added. "You know this is the perfect dress to dazzle nasty Ted and make Marigold sweat. Just put it on."

They were standing in the nonbridal side of the store. Taryn and Shelby were sitting and watching the exchange with great interest.

"I'm thinking we should take bets," Shelby said.

"I want to know which dress she's wearing so I can flash some jewelry," Taryn told them. "I brought sapphires, like Isabel said, but I also have diamonds and pearls."

Because Taryn was nothing if not fashion prepared.

Madeline looked at her friends, then back at the dress. "Thanks," she said, taking it from Isabel. "I owe you."

"Yes, I know."

Isabel took a seat and waved toward the dressing rooms. "Go on. Dazzle us."

Madeline retreated to the dressing room and pulled off the plain black dress she'd worn for work. She changed out black tights for sheer stockings, then shimmied into a shapewear slip that kept things from jiggling too much. She stepped into the dress and pulled it up, then walked out of the dressing room.

Shelby was on her feet immediately.

"You look great," she said, coming up behind her and doing the zipper, then the little hook and eye at the top. "The color is amazing on you."

"Thanks."

Madeline walked over to the mirror and studied herself. She'd already redone her makeup and her hair was up in hot rollers. In five more minutes, she would take them out, finger comb her hair, then spray it into submission.

Taryn nodded. "It's a good one. I have several shoe options, but I think I know what will work." She pulled out a box and opened the top. Inside was a pair of high-heeled pumps in a shimmering kind of silver.

Madeline looked closer and saw the shoes were covered with crystals.

"Christian Louboutin. The crystals are hand-set Swarovski."

"Of course they are," Madeline murmured. "Just tell me this. Are they worth more than a thousand dollars?"

Taryn rolled her eyes. "All I hear is a buzzing sound. Take them, Madeline. They'll look fantastic with the dress."

Madeline tucked her hands behind her back. "No way."

Taryn's brows drew together. "They're just shoes. You're my friend and I love you. I also dislike Marigold and Ted. Take the shoes."

Taryn could be stern and determined but she was also incredibly generous with her friends. Madeline picked up the ridiculously high heels and sat down before slipping them on her feet.

They were stunning. "I'm not sure I can stand," Madeline admitted. "But I don't know if I care."

"Exactly. Just sit and look beautiful." Taryn eyed her. "You know, the sapphires are going to be too matchy-matchy. Let's do diamonds."

She dug through her tote and pulled out a couple of Tiffany boxes. Inside one was a pair of simple diamond studs. In the other was a diamond pendant necklace.

Shelby took the necklace and fastened it around her neck. "Just hope that at midnight this doesn't turn into a pumpkin, because that could hurt."

Taryn held out the earrings. "I insist. Come on. You know you want to."

"You have to." Tears started down Isabel's cheeks.

Madeline hurried to her side. "What's wrong?"

"Nothing. I'm pregnant. It's a beautiful moment, so

I'm crying. Put on the damn earrings, would you? Then go do your hair so we can ooh and aah over you."

Madeline did as she asked, returning less than five minutes later. She stepped into the stunning shoes, then made a slow circle.

Everyone nodded and applauded. "You'll devastate Marigold for sure," Isabel said. "And that jerk Ted."

Taryn rose and put her arm around Isabel. "I'm going to get her home. I think she needs a couple of hugs from her husband."

"I need wine," Isabel said with a sigh. "Only a few more months until that happens."

"Unless she plans to breastfeed," Shelby murmured.

"I can hear you," Isabel yelled as she and Taryn left.

Madeline slipped out of the shoes. No way she was going to wear them a second longer than necessary. She needed to save her high-heel time for actually walking into the restaurant.

"Where are you meeting them?" Shelby asked.

"Henri's." It was a five-star restaurant, up at the Gold Rush resort.

"Nice."

Shelby helped her tidy up the boxes and bags. Madeline figured she would come in a half hour early in the morning and collect all Taryn's things, then return them to her. As for the soon-to-be-marked-down dress, she was going to have to think about buying it. Returning it after wearing it seemed tacky.

"Are you excited about your date?" Shelby asked.

"It's not a date. It's a mercy dinner. Jonny's helping me out. Nothing more."

Her friend nodded knowingly. "That's a lot of energy for a nondate."

"I know. I can't help it. It's just he's so..."

"Jonny Blaze-like?"

"Yes. When I'm around him, it's hard to see anything beyond the blinding light of his appeal."

"As long as you're not getting in over your head," Shelby teased. Then her humor faded. "Do I have to worry about you?"

"No." Madeline held up a hand. "I swear, I'm fine. Am I attracted to him? Of course. I'm breathing and into guys. It's inevitable. At the same time I'm clear on who he is and what I want in life. Someone to love. Someone to be with for the rest of my life."

"That could be him."

"Do you really see him falling for someone like me and settling down in Fool's Gold?"

Shelby looked at her and nodded. "Absolutely. Why not?"

Madeline laughed. "Which is why we're friends. You're very sweet, but full of it."

"I disagree. Why not you?"

An interesting question, Madeline thought when her friend had left. One to which she didn't have an answer.

At a minute before six, she slipped on the infamous shoes and reached for her coat. Jonny walked into the store wearing a tailored suit that fit him perfectly. Most likely handmade, Madeline thought as her throat went dry. He'd shaved and looked good enough to be on a movie poster. Probably a good thing, considering his profession.

Her body reacted in the usual way. Tingles and heating, with a bit of breathlessness thrown in for fun.

"Hi," she managed.

"Hi, yourself."

He walked toward her, then circled around her, before leaning in and kissing her cheek. "Wow. You're stunning. More beautiful than usual, which isn't easy."

Talk about a great compliment, she thought with a smile. "You're very shiny yourself. Ted and Marigold won't know what hit them."

He glanced down at her shoes. "Christian Louboutin?"

She raised one foot. "Should I be scared you know who designed these?"

"The red soles are well-known."

"Maybe in your circles. If I hadn't read the name on the box, I wouldn't have had a clue."

"Part of your charm," he told her.

Really? He thought she had charm? Was that the same as being charming?

He took her hand. "Come on. We have people to dazzle."

She drew in a breath for courage, reminded herself that, unlike Cinderella, she could stay out past midnight and not turn into a pumpkin, then promised herself that she was going to have a good time, no matter what. For one evening she got to pretend she was on a date with famous actor Jonny Blaze. Even better, she really *was* going out with a guy she liked. He might just be doing her a favor, but a girl could dream.

The drive up to the resort went by more quickly than she'd thought it would. Madeline found herself growing more and more nervous. By the time Jonny parked by the valet and she was stepping out of his SUV, she found it difficult to breathe.

What if this was a mistake? What if Ted and Marigold figured out it was all fake? Because they would. No one could possibly believe Jonny was interested in her.

So they were all going to laugh and point and she would be left humiliated.

She glanced around for an escape, but before she could plot a course she could manage in Taryn's borrowed shoes, Jonny put his hand on the small of her back and guided her into the hotel.

The decorations were festive, the music soft. Madeline felt as if everyone was staring. They weren't, but she still felt awkward. And with awkward came the babble.

"My parents used to bring me here for special events," she told him. "It was a big deal to have dinner at Henri's. Some of the decorations in the main lobby go back generations."

She pointed to the massive tree stretching up over twenty feet. "The tree skirt is handmade and an heirloom. There's an actual insurance policy on it, which is crazy, right? Some of the decorations date back to the 1800s." She swallowed. "Oh, wait. I just said that."

She was about to launch into a detailed explanation of the original mercury glass when Jonny pulled her into a small alcove. He put one hand on her waist and lightly stroked her cheek with the other.

"Don't worry," he said quietly. "You're the prize that got away. That's why he wants to have dinner with you. Because every time he's hoping to find out you're not all that and it doesn't happen. You're beautiful, you're sweet, you're smart and he's an idiot."

The words were magical. She hoped they were real, but even if he was just acting, she didn't care. She suddenly felt taller and thinner and a whole lot more capable of handling Ted and Marigold.

"Thank you."

"You're welcome." His gaze dropped to her mouth. "Damn lipstick," he muttered, then took her hand and drew her back into the hallway.

Wow, she thought happily. Bringing him along had been one of her best ideas. Only she sort of remembered it had been his idea, which made him even better to have around. Smart *and* pretty.

They reached the entrance to the dining room. Before she could give her name to the hostess, Ted and Marigold walked up.

Ted was tall and good-looking. Madeline had always thought he was swoon-worthy. But somehow his star seemed to burn a little less bright this year. She knew she had Jonny to thank for that. Marigold was also tall and willowy. A beautiful redhead with pale skin and wide, brown eyes.

Next to her, Madeline always felt dowdy. Not tonight, she told herself. In her borrowed finery, she was a princess for sure. Or, at the very least, a successful business-woman out for an evening.

"Madeline," Ted said, glancing from her to Jonny. "You brought a date."

The tone of surprise was a tiny bit insulting, but she overlooked that. Because she didn't just have *a* date. She had a killer date.

"I thought a foursome would be more fun," she said easily. "Hello, Ted." She leaned in and they hugged. "Marigold." She turned and smiled at Jonny. "I'd like you to meet friends of mine. Jonny, this is Ted and Marigold."

Jonny shook hands with both of them. "The old flame. I appreciate the chance to size up what used to be the competition."

Madeline knew it was probably wrong, but she'd de-liberately not used any last names. She wanted Ted and Marigold to stare, to wonder. She wanted to see the exact moment they—

"Jonny Blaze?" Marigold asked, her voice a squeak. "Ohmygod! You're Jonny Blaze." Marigold lunged for him, stopping inches before engulfing him. She cleared her throat and stepped back. "I can't believe it. What are you doing here?"

Jonny reached for Madeline's hand and brought it to

his mouth where he lightly kissed her knuckles. "I'm with the beautiful blonde."

"I don't understand."

Marigold's look of confusion was as funny as it was insulting. Madeline told herself to enjoy the moment and not worry that Marigold couldn't grasp that she and Jonny were a couple. It wasn't as if Madeline would have believed it, either.

"You're dating Jonny Blaze?" Ted asked, sounding as perplexed as his wife.

"So it seems," Madeline said, then turned to the hostess. "Would you please show us to our table?"

It took nearly a half hour for the evening to return to something like normal. The four of them were seated and ordered cocktails. Marigold kept staring at Jonny with a combination of disbelief and hunger. Madeline understood both emotions but she found the other woman's wide-eyed stare a little off-putting.

For his part, Jonny took the weirdness in stride. He kept the conversation flowing and made sure to touch Madeline's arm or hand, just like an attentive date would. It was nice. Tempting. The fact that it wasn't real didn't bother her in the least.

"How's work?" Ted asked Madeline. "You're still in

retail, right?" He turned to Jonny. "I'm the local weather guy up in Washington state."

"Seattle?" Jonny asked, even though Madeline was pretty sure he already knew the answer.

"Ah, no. Yakima. It's a small town, east of the Cascade mountains."

"I see."

Marigold leaned toward him. "I was a model," she said eagerly.

"Yes. Madeline told me."

The words were simple enough, but there was something in his tone that implied being a model wasn't all that. Marigold frowned, as if not sure what had gone wrong.

Jonny laced his fingers with Madeline. "My girl here is part-owner of Paper Moon. They sell wedding gowns. I think what I like best about what she does is how she makes dreams come true. Women go in with an idea of how their wedding day should be and Madeline makes that happen. People remember their weddings for the rest of their lives."

Ted and Marigold exchanged a look.

"Ah, right," Ted said awkwardly. "It's good you found something you liked." His voice became confidential. "Madeline had a little trouble figuring out what she wanted to do. College, culinary school. I know I'm forgetting a few disasters."

Madeline thought about pointing out he would fall firmly in the disaster category, but knew there was no way to say that without sounding bitchy and she was still determined to come out of the evening as the victor.

"I admire people who don't settle," Jonny told him. "People who aren't afraid to keep trying. Most of us take what we can get. A smaller job because it's safe. But a brave few keep searching for what's right, and when they find it, they hang on."

It took Madeline a second to realize he was talking about her. She stared at him.

"I didn't—" she began.

He cut her off with a quick kiss. "You did. It's one of the things I like best about you."

The rest of the meal passed in a blur. Madeline talked in what she hoped were all the right places and laughed at the jokes, but everything had gotten kind of confusing. She wasn't sure what was real and what was pretend. What she knew for sure was that Jonny was even more charming than she'd thought possible. He was attentive and funny, and when he looked at her with what felt a lot like desire, she melted. If this was acting, imagine how powerful he could be if it was real. No woman would stand a chance.

The waiter spoke as he cleared their dinner plates. "We have a special dessert for the holidays. Chocolate waffles with homemade peppermint ice cream and a special sauce the chef has created."

Marigold sighed. "That sounds scrumptious, but I couldn't possibly—"

"We'll have one for the table," Jonny said smoothly.

"It does sound delicious," Madeline told him.

He put his arm around her. "That's my girl." He looked at Marigold. "What are your plans for the holidays?" he asked.

"We'll visit my family. We do it every year. I'm from a small town in Iowa. What about you?"

"My sister's getting married the day after Christmas. Madeline's been helping me with that." He smiled at her. "I couldn't have managed it without her. She's taking care of all the details."

Ted sat up straighter. "That's it! She's working for you. You hired her to plan your sister's wedding. She's not a date, she's an employee."

He sounded both triumphant and relieved. Madeline wasn't sure what to say in return, while next to her, Jonny tensed.

"I'm not paying Madeline," he said, his tone low. "She doesn't work for me."

She thought about their arrangement. She had refused money. She'd wanted the experience and being paid had just felt wrong.

"I have a job," she told Ted. "I wasn't looking for part-time work. Actually, Mayor Marsha's the one who brought us together. Jonny needed help and she suggested me. I was happy to step in." She smiled at him. "When you think about it, it's a very strange way to meet."

"But a great story."

Madeline shifted closer to him, but looked at the couple across the table. "Ginger is Jonny's younger sister. She's getting her PhD. Talk about the smartest person in the room. But she's totally adorable. I'm so happy I can help her. The wedding's going to be lovely."

Ted looked at his wife, then back at her. "You're really with him."

Madeline shrugged.

"I don't…" He nodded. "Okay. Well, I hope you'll be happy together."

Madeline shivered slightly in Jonny's SUV. He had the heat on high and the seat heaters going, but it was well below freezing and snowing. Her light wrap, while pretty, didn't exactly warm her.

The wine helped. And the lemon drop she'd had as her cocktail. But still—it was winter. She was looking forward to getting into her warmest pajamas and climbing into bed.

"That was the strangest dinner ever," she said. "I don't know what to think."

"You're not going to hear from Ted again."

"You don't think so?"

"No. He had something to prove and now he knows he can't."

"Do you think we hurt their feelings?"

Jonny glanced at her. "How long have they been coming here?"

"Three years."

"And at the end of every dinner, you feel worse about yourself and wish you didn't have to see them again."

"Uh-huh."

"And you're still worried about their feelings?"

"I can't help it."

"That makes you a good person."

She supposed she should just go with that. Not about being a good person, but that for once Ted and Marigold hadn't been able to beat up on her. Of course, a case could be made that she'd allowed them to do it, which made everything confusing.

She turned to Jonny. "Thank you for tonight. For taking me and being my date and saying such nice things about me."

He pulled up in front of her house and turned off the engine. "You're welcome."

She got out of the car and started toward her front door. He walked with her.

"You're a really good actor," she continued. "Poor Marigold. I think she wanted to get you in her to-go box. I almost felt sorry for her." They reached her front porch and she turned to him.

"You're a fun date," she said with a grin. "You can turn on the charm. I know it was just for their sake, by the way. Don't worry that I'm going to turn into stalker girl or anything."

"I never thought you would."

His eyes were so beautiful, she thought as she stared at his face. And while the outside package was darned appealing, she had to admit there was something about the inner man that worked for her, too. The more she was around him, the more she liked him.

She shivered.

"You're freezing," he said. "Let's get you inside."

She fumbled for her key, only then wondering why he'd walked her to her door instead of waiting in his car. She opened the door and stepped inside. She turned, ready to say good-night. Only Jonny hadn't waited on the porch. Instead, he'd followed her inside.

He closed the front door, took her bag from her and put it on the small table in her entry alcove. Then he put his arms around her and drew her close.

If she'd been with any other man, she would have thought he was going to kiss her. Only there was no way that he would—

His mouth was firm and warm and brushed against hers in the most delightful way possible. Madeline battled surprise and desire as the kiss went on for two heartbeats, then three. She raised her arms, not quite sure what to do with them. Putting them on his body seemed the most logical thing. That was what you did when you kissed. You hugged back.

So she let her hands settle on him. One rested on his shoulder, the other on his side. She felt the muscles in his body and the warmth. Her shoes made her a little wobbly, but that was okay because he was nice to cling to.

She liked the feel of his lips on hers. She liked how they fit together. Tingles danced all through her, and even with her eyes closed she saw the bolts of lightning all around them.

Actor's magic, she told herself firmly even as his tongue lightly brushed against her lower lip.

She parted for him, not sure what to expect. He deepened the kiss. His tongue teased hers and, with every stroke, she leaned into him.

Wanting grew, as did heat. Suddenly she wasn't cold anymore. She was trembling and ready and determined not to act like a fool, even though she wanted to.

He drew back and looked into her eyes. "I wasn't acting," he said, just before he released her and walked out the door.

❧ NINE ❧

JONNY RAISED THE BARBELL ONE last time and held it for
a count of ten. He would have gone for twenty, but his
arms were shaking and he didn't have a spotter. No way
he wanted to end up pinned. Although the rescue video
would make a splash on *TMZ*, he thought humorously as
he set the barbell back in the stand and sucked in a breath.

He knew that some actors took their downtime
seriously—getting out of shape and putting on weight—
then worked hard to get ripped again when filming
started. He preferred a more balanced approached. It
was easier to stay fit than get fit. He was willing to eat
pasta and the occasional cookie, but for the most part,
he stayed with his regular fitness routine. When he was
about two months from filming, he got more disciplined,
but didn't have to hit the gym five hours a day to get in
fighting condition.

He stood and grabbed his water bottle. After downing

half of it, he headed for the treadmill. He would run his second two miles before hitting the shower, then drive into town. He had some more ideas for the wedding to discuss with Madeline.

As he pushed the button to start his treadmill program, he allowed himself to think about their recent dinner. She'd been a fun date—no surprise there. He'd liked spending time with her. She laughed easily, which was a quality he liked in a woman. She was caring, sexy. All qualities designed to get him wondering about possibilities. If things were different...if *he* were different.

He could see himself getting serious about her. Ginger had liked her, as well, and that was important to him. Around Madeline, he could relax and be himself. Whatever she'd felt about him being Jonny Blaze, Action Star, had quickly faded. Now he was just some guy she knew.

Except he wasn't just some guy and being with him would bring challenges she couldn't begin to imagine. He'd seen the disaster serious relationships with someone like him could be. Not a very nice thing to do to someone he liked. So he was left with wanting but not having.

Like the kiss. He'd left her on her front door, as if he was some freshman in high school. He'd wanted to do more. Have more. He'd wanted to hold her and make love with her. To please her and be with her. He'd wanted what any man kissing Madeline would want.

He stepped on the treadmill and set the program. He chose one of the more challenging ones, hoping it would distract him. But seventeen minutes later, when he'd finished, he was panting, sweating and still thinking about Madeline.

As he returned to the house and headed for the shower, he thought about what Ginger had said. That he used his fame to hide. If it was true—he was actually afraid to be in a relationship rather than protecting the person he claimed to care about—then the solution was easy. He would just move forward and force himself to face his fears. Which sounded plenty easy but he suspected would be difficult to do.

Too many questions, he thought, stripping off his workout gear. The bottom line was he wanted to see Madeline and he only knew one way to make that happen.

Less than an hour later, he drove into town. The snow was heavier than it had been in the past few days. It piled up on the road. He'd spent enough time in the mountains that he was confident about his driving and his SUV's ability to handle the weather. He turned onto Brian Lane and found parking, then got out and headed for Paper Moon.

When he stepped inside, he saw that Madeline was with a customer. The willowy brunette stood with her hands on her hips. Her posture was defiant, her chin jutted out. By contrast, Madeline's shoulders were relaxed, but Jonny saw the tension in the edges of her polite smile.

"I can contact the designer," she was saying. "But you did sign the order form and it clearly states that the veils aren't returnable."

"This isn't what I ordered," the brunette insisted, her voice boarding on shrill. "Why can't you get that through your head?" She sighed heavily. "Everyone is so stupid. I don't get that. It's a simple thing. I want the veil I ordered."

Madeline nodded. "Of course you do. And as you can see by the picture attached to the order, this is that veil. Down to the family coat of arms you requested be embroidered on the edges."

The bride looked at the picture and then back at the veil draped across a narrow table. "They don't look the same at all."

Even he could see they were identical. He had no idea why the bridezilla was trying to get out of the order. She still wore an engagement ring, and from the paperwork scattered around, it seemed she'd bought a dress. His gaze drifted to the order for the veil. It had been eight thousand dollars. That was a lot for some lace and a few silk flowers. He supposed the custom coat of arms had something to do with it. Maybe the bride had been told to rein in the spending. He could respect that. But trying to screw Madeline over a veil she had no hope of selling to someone else was wrong.

He crossed to the two women.

"Sorry I'm late," he told Madeline, even though they didn't have an appointment. He smiled at the bride. "Hi. Am I interrupting? I'm Jonny Blaze." He held out his hand. "Nice to meet you."

"Ella," the other woman said, her eyes widening. "Oh, my God. Did you say Jonny Blaze?"

He gave a self-deprecating shrug. "That would be me. Are you getting your dress here?"

Ella nodded. "I am."

"Good choice. My sister is, too." He winked at Madeline. "But that needs to be our secret, okay? We don't want to have to deal with the press."

"I won't say anything," Ella promised, still looking stunned. "I can't believe you're here. In this town. I live in Sacramento, but getting wedding dresses from Paper Moon is kind of a family tradition."

"Nice," he said, and picked up a couple of the pictures. "Your dress?"

"Uh-huh."

"Beautiful." He set them on the table, then nodded at the veil. "May I?"

"Sure."

What he knew about wedding veils wouldn't max out a tweet, but he was an actor and he'd worked on enough period movies to have spent time with costume designers. He knew how to fake his way through almost anything clothing related.

"Stunning," he declared after studying the delicate lace. While it wasn't anything he would have picked for his sister, he could appreciate the craftsmanship. "Handmade. You can tell it's special." He leaned in. "Are those crests on the edge of the lace?"

"The family coat of arms," Madeline murmured.

He looked at Ella. "Smart girl. A unique detail no one else will have. You've taken a very traditional, almost ordinary accessory and personalized in a way that not only complements your dress, but gives you a link to both the past and present in your family. Your kids are going to love hearing about your veil."

Ella blushed. "It was just an idea. I had to order this specially. It took months."

"You're smart to wait for quality. Too many people are

impatient." He flashed her his best smile. "Congratulations." He put down the veil.

"Would you mind taking a picture with me?" she asked.

"I'd love to. Will you wear the veil?"

"What? Oh, that's a great idea." She turned to Madeline. "Help me put it on?"

Madeline flashed him a grateful look, then helped Ella secure the veil. Jonny took several pictures with her, then signed an autograph for her fiancé. Ten minutes later Ella and her veil left the store, but not before the bride thanked Madeline for helping her get exactly what she'd always wanted.

When the door closed behind her, Madeline turned to him. "I can't decide if you're gifted or the devil."

"Can I be both?"

She leaned against the table and sighed. "Thank you. Things were getting out of hand."

When she didn't say any more than that, Jonny realized she wouldn't talk about a customer with him. But he'd seen enough to fill in the details. Having to eat a customer order that big would have devastated the profits for the month. Maybe the quarter. Paper Moon was successful but still a small business. He would guess the margins were small.

"I promise not to order a custom veil for Ginger," he told her.

"There isn't time, but either way, thank you for that, as well." She picked up the paperwork and started for her office. "What brings you into town today?"

You.

He only thought the word rather than speaking it, but it echoed in his head all the same. As they sat across from each other in her small, plain office, he saw the way she glanced at him, then away. There was a slight stain of color on her cheeks. While Ella had been around, Madeline had been completely professional. Now that they were alone, he liked to think that she was remembering what had happened between them the previous night.

And while that was nice to dwell on, there was still her question to answer.

"The toys," he said, mentioning the first reasonable topic that came to mind. "I want to donate them to the toy drive, but they're not ready. They need to be painted."

"Oh, I'd forgotten. They're wood?"

He nodded. "I have some child-safe paints but there's no way I can get everything done in time. Do you know someone I could hire?"

She wrinkled her nose. "That's not how we do things

around here," she told him. "You don't hire someone else. You have a paint party."

"A what?"

"A paint party. I put the word out and a dozen or so people show up for a few hours to get the job done. If we need more hands than that, I simply call more people."

"No way."

She smiled. "Way. How many toys are you talking about?"

"Close to fifty. Want to come see them? You haven't been to the house. You should probably look at where the wedding is going to be."

Did he sound casual? He wanted to. He didn't want her to know how his palms were suddenly sweaty. He swore silently, trying to remember that he'd met heads of state and dated supermodels, not to mention a princess or two. So why was he nervous about inviting Madeline to his place?

"You're right," she told him with a laugh. "I can't believe I haven't seen where the wedding is going to be. And here I thought I was doing a good job. Yes, I need to see your house and the toys. When's a good time?"

"What about now?"

He expected her to tell him she couldn't possibly. Instead, she stood. "I have a free afternoon. Let me tell Rosalind that I'm going to be gone a couple of hours."

"You'll need your coat. It's snowing."

Madeline sat in the passenger's seat of Jonny's SUV and told herself that there was no way the snow was more sparkly than usual. That it was just her imagination. Something that until she'd met him, she'd never had any problem controlling.

Now, as they drove up the mountain, she watched the magical flakes dance and twirl as they fell to the ground. Holiday music played from the speakers. She was alone with a handsome man who made her laugh and it was snowing. Did moments get more perfect than this?

"Do you have a lot of clients like Ella?" he asked.

"Not usually. Sometimes a bride doesn't like the dress when it comes in. We try to work with her on that. There's usually a time crunch, so it's often faster to have the gown altered than to start over. You'd be amazed at what a great seamstress can do. A veil is different." She looked at him. "Thanks for your help."

He raised an eyebrow. "I have no idea what you're talking about."

She laughed. "Yes, you do. You were great. I half expected you to start talking about Princess Grace or Kate Middleton."

"I was holding those two in reserve. You never start by playing your princess card. Do you think she'll be happy with the veil?"

"I hope so. If she changes her mind again and brings it back, I'll have to figure out what to do." Which was a problem for another day.

"Have you heard from Ted?" he asked.

Madeline did her best to hold in a giggle. "There was a brief thank-you note in my email this morning. He said to thank you for dinner and he wished me a happy holiday. I have a feeling you're right. There isn't going to be any more contact from Ted in my future."

"You okay with that?"

"I couldn't be happier."

"He's not the one who got away?"

She considered the question. "Maybe a year ago I would have said he was, but not anymore. I think maybe you're right about him not letting go. I can't figure out why, though. He wasn't in love with me. If he was, he wouldn't have married Marigold. But he refused to just disappear." She glanced at Jonny. "I confess I'm not very good at staying friends with my exes. I suppose if I were a better person I would."

"Not necessarily. Some people don't like to let go. Others can be friends with everyone."

He turned off the main highway onto a small road. The snow fell more heavily but the windshield wipers were able to keep up.

"I've never been out here," she told him. "I've been to the Nicholson Ranch a few times." She grinned. "Zane was very hot in high school."

Jonny sighed. "I've heard he was voted the guy girls wanted to lose their virginity to four years in a row."

"I'm shocked you know that."

"I'm shocked there was a poll. Seriously? I expect better of your gender."

"Have you seen Zane? He's the classic silent-cowboy type. Strong and brooding. Teenage girls love a good brooder."

Jonny glanced at her. "You know he's happily married, right?"

"Yes, I do, and my crush is long over."

"You're sure?"

"Completely."

She told herself he was teasing. Or maybe even flirting. But there was no way he was genuinely concerned. Or interested. Still, a girl could dream and she planned on having a very good night.

They drove up a long driveway. The snow was about six inches deep and still coming down.

"Do you plow this?" she asked. "You'd need a truck and a plow attachment."

Jonny shook his head. "A guy comes through when we have weather. Having a service is the only way to keep the driveway open when I travel."

He slowed down and drove carefully. Madeline noticed they didn't swerve at all. Looked like he was good for more than action sequences on the big screen.

When they reached the main house, he parked in front. The ranch-style home sprawled out as if it had been added to over the years. There was a wide front porch and a big double door. The house wasn't new, but it looked welcoming. Especially with the heavy dusting of snow.

"The toys are out back in one of the barns," he told her. "Wait and I'll come around. It's going to be slippery out there."

Because he wanted her to be safe. An excellent quality in a man. But if she slipped, wouldn't he try to catch her? They could fall together in tangle of arms and legs. In real life, that would be desperately cold, but this was her fantasy. She could ignore everything except how it would feel to have him hold her close and—

"Ready?" he asked as he opened her door.

"Um, sure."

She stepped out and immediately sank into about eight inches of snow. It was cold, but also beautiful. The trees looked like something out of a Christmas card.

"Around here," he said, taking her hand and leading her past the house.

Once they were between the house and the garage, it was easier to walk. Then they were out in the open again and the snow drifted down steadily. She saw two big barns.

"My workshop is in there," he said, pointing to the closer one. "The other has the open area for the wedding."

"Let's look at the toys first."

He guided her to a side door. They walked into a foyer with two doors beyond. The right one led to a huge workout room. Seriously, it was the size of a professional gym. There was every kind of equipment imaginable and a few she couldn't begin to place. No wonder he looked as good as he did.

The left door was partially closed. Jonny pushed it open and motioned for her to go first. He clicked on the lights as she stepped over the threshold.

"It used to be the ranch workshop," he said. "It's bigger than I need, but I like the windows."

Despite the snowfall, light spilled into the room. There were a couple of long workbenches, two desks and lots of cabinets. Everything was obviously cared for but worn. Tools were hung neatly on a peg board. Carved toys filled open shelves.

She hadn't known what to expect. Maybe some primitively honed bears or a shell of a car. Instead, the toys were smooth and detailed. The dinosaurs had carved scales and the cars had wheels that not only turned but had tread on their tires. One of the trucks could be loaded with blocks. She touched the side of a castle.

"These are amazing," she breathed. "They're so beautiful. They must take hours."

"There's a lot of downtime on a movie set."

"Apparently." She looked at him. "You're talented."

"I had a good teacher. He was very patient with me. These are nothing compared to what he can do. But I enjoy making them."

He showed her the paint he'd bought, along with brushes. "I didn't know where to start," he admitted. "What colors to use. That's not my thing."

The paint was all labeled as approved by the FDA, so food-level safe. Perfect for kids.

"I can make some calls," she told him. "There are a lot of creative people in town. If we got everyone together for an afternoon, we could get everything painted in a few hours. Are you sure you want to donate these?"

"Yes. Better for kids to play with them than for them to just sit here."

"They're going to be wonderful."

They went back outside. The wind was much stronger than it had been. They went into the second barn. There were a couple of bathrooms, but otherwise it was one big open space. She took pictures with her phone.

"I've already reserved the tables and chairs," she said as she turned to get the room from every angle. "I know there are plenty of twinkle lights. The lady at Plants for the Planet mentioned some large potted plants we could rent. It'll take me a few days to get with everyone to figure out the best layout. But the room's nice and big. That gives us a lot to work with."

She walked to the far end. "We could set up the ceremony here. With only forty or fifty guests, we need... what? Five rows of chairs? Ten across with a center aisle? That won't take much space. I wonder if Dellina can help me get some screens or something to divide the space. I'll text her and ask."

She took more pictures, before turning to him.

"I have what I need. Thanks for showing me all this."

"You're welcome."

He opened the door and was blasted by a gust of wind and plenty of snow. Even from several feet back, she felt the cold.

They made their way toward the house. Just in the half hour or so since they'd arrived, another inch or two lay on the ground. When they reached his SUV, she saw the entire front end was buried.

Jonny shook his head. "I'm going to have to dig this out. You go inside and get warm." He handed her his house keys, then went to the garage.

Madeline let herself into the house. She entered through a mudroom that led to the kitchen. Although the urge to explore was strong, she forced herself to stay by the mudroom. Jonny trusted her. She wouldn't take advantage of that.

Twenty minutes later, he joined her. Snow coated his head and both sides of his coat.

"It's coming down faster than I can dig out the car," he told her. "I should have paid more attention to the conditions before I brought you here. I'm sorry. You're going to have to stay until the storm passes."

The words bounced around in her brain. At first they didn't make any sense and then they did. Stay. Here. In his house. Alone. The two of them.

Merry Christmas to her, she thought, trying not to break into the happy dance.

Jonny took off his coat and gloves, then moved in front of her. "I didn't plan this, Madeline."

"I didn't think you had."

"I don't want you to be nervous. I'm not putting the moves on you."

Darn. He didn't have to actually come out and say that, she thought. He could have let her wonder...and hope. Unless he knew about her crush. Oh, no. Did he? Was he right this minute thinking she was thrilled about being snowed in with him and dreading the time he had to spend with her?

"Of course not," she said brightly. "Why would I think that? We're friends. I'm helping with your sister's wedding. Nothing more."

She hoped she sounded totally sincere and disinterested in him in that way. Because the alternative was humiliating. Honestly, if there hadn't been two feet of snow on the ground, she would have started walking home right that second.

Jonny motioned for her to lead the way out of the mudroom, only to put his hand on her forearm when she started to move. He turned her until she faced him again. One corner of his mouth turned up.

"Nothing will happen tonight," he repeated.

She did her best not to wince.

"But that doesn't mean I won't be tempted."

❧ TEN ❧

THERE WAS NOTHING LIKE A man confessing to wild sexual desire to brighten up a girl's day, Madeline thought as she tried to come up with something witty to say in response. "Thank you" seemed really lame and "Me, too" was just too, well, dangerous. Because while wanting him was pretty safe, she wasn't sure what would happen if she actually had him. Even counting the Ted debacle, she'd never been one to sleep around. For her, being that intimate had meant she had crossed an emotional threshold. Maybe not to the point of being in love, but darned close.

She liked Jonny a lot, and yes, there were plenty of tingles, zips and zings. But they weren't about anything real. They couldn't be. Not only did he have commitment issues, he was famous. And she was little more than a shopgirl.

"I don't know what to say," she admitted when the silence had stretched out far too long.

"How about a tour of the house? That will give you plenty to talk about."

"I like a man with a plan."

"That's me."

They went into the kitchen.

"Someone's done some work," she said, thinking about the age of the ranch house compared with the modern kitchen.

There was a large island with a built-in wine fridge at one end, some kind of fancy granite countertop and beautiful wood cabinets that stretched to the ceiling. A huge farm sink sat in front of a bay window. Right now all she could see was semidarkness and snow but she would bet that when the weather was nice, the view was amazing.

"I had the kitchen gutted," Jonny admitted. "It was the original one, and while I love avocado tile as much as the next guy, I figured it was time for a change."

"You flew in a decorator?"

He nodded. "The construction team was local, though."

"Hendrix Construction?"

"You know them?"

"They're one of the founding families in town, so yes." She smiled. "They do good work."

"I agree."

Off the kitchen was a dining room with a rock wall and a fireplace. It was open on both sides and beyond that was the family room.

Here there hadn't been many changes, she thought, taking in the worn stone and the beautiful beam mantel. The table and twelve chairs looked well-worn, but happy. Maybe a strange description for furniture, but Madeline was sticking with it.

"Some of the furniture came with the house," Jonny told her. "This dining room set and a lot of the wood pieces."

Madeline knew that old Reilly Konopka had moved to Florida to be near his kids and grandkids, but that until he'd sold, his family had owned the ranch for about fifty years.

"There are a lot of memories in this house," she murmured.

"I know. I like that. The history. There's a good feeling here. Ginger likes the house."

He showed her the family room. The furniture there was mostly new, but well done with a beige upholstered sectional and a couple of leather chairs. A big Christmas tree stood in the corner. It was artificial and looked professionally done. Beautiful, she thought, but without the charm of one that had been decorated with ornaments that might be worn but were also filled with emotional significance.

"The guest rooms are this way."

The house was kind of U-shaped, with the kitchen and family room at the base of the U. They went down the right hallway, past an office. Jonny pushed open a door that led into a comfortable room with a queen-size bed, a dresser and an attached bathroom.

There were neatly folded towels on a bench and fluffy pillows on the bed.

"I use a service," he admitted. "They clean and keep things ready."

"It's nice," she said, wondering where the master was but not about to ask. The situation was a little awkward. Interesting, but strange. She was both nervous and excited, which left her feeling that she could easily do something foolish, like walk into a wall or say something ridiculous.

She told herself to relax, that she and Jonny had spent plenty of time together. If they ran out of conversation, there was always the wedding. They could discuss linens and music selections.

They went back into the kitchen. He showed her the pantry off the kitchen. In addition to shelves and prep sink, there was a large upright freezer. She opened it and started to laugh. He moved closer and looked over her shoulder.

"People dropped off some casseroles," he told her.

"I recognize some of the serving dishes, which means I know what's inside. We're very big on casseroles here in town. There's even a casserole cook-off."

"I'll have to be in town that weekend," he said.

She raised her eyebrows. "On purpose?"

"Hey, I grew up with a single dad. Anything home-made is my favorite."

"A man with low culinary standards. Tell me again why women aren't lining up to marry you?"

He chuckled. "I leave socks on the floor."

"Oh, well, then. That explains it." She studied the various selections. "How about lasagna?"

"Sounds good."

She pulled out the dish, unwrapped it and set it on the counter to start defrosting. She would finish that process in the microwave later, but first went back into the pantry to check for other ingredients.

Whoever did the shopping had made sure he had the basics. She found plenty of fresh vegetables, along with spices, flour and sugar.

"Do you have a generator?" she asked.

"Sure. Whole house. If we lose power, it kicks on in twenty seconds. Why?"

"I think I'll make cookies." She found a couple of packages of yeast. "And maybe some garlic rolls. Oh, and salad dressing." There weren't any lemons, but he had fresh garlic and white vinegar. She could whip up a flavored ranch dressing easily. "If you have milk."

"I don't have any recipes."

"You don't need them. I can do this from memory." She handed him vinegar, garlic and the flour. "You've met my mother. Cooking is a big deal to her, so she taught me. Stand back and be impressed."

"I already am."

Thirty minutes later peanut butter cookies were in the oven. She set Jonny to work, washing out the cute elephant-shaped cookie jar she'd spotted in the pantry.

While he took care of that, she added flour to the mixture in the bowl. When all the flour was incorporated, she dropped it onto the counter and began kneading.

"When that timer goes off, I'll need you to take out the first batch of cookies and put in the second," she told him.

"Just say when."

"You're very agreeable."

"I don't have a problem being your sous chef. Home-cooked meals are a treat."

Based on the frozen dinners in his freezer and the take-out containers in his refrigerator, she knew he wasn't lying.

"You could have a chef or something," she said.

He put the cookie jar on the counter. "Not my style. I'm not the staff type."

That was true. She would guess most stars at his level had a personal assistant, but he didn't. She knew his manager and her people took care of some things, but the rest he did himself.

"In the summer I barbecue a lot," he said as he sat in a stool at the island. "I grill a mean steak."

"You're such a guy."

He winked. "I am."

"My dad and brother both love to barbecue, too. But put them in front of a stove and they're lost. Which makes no sense to me. A gas stove still has fire."

"But it's indoors. Not the same at all."

"Uh-huh. Why do I know that's a trick to keep women cooking for you?"

"Never."

"Right."

She put the kneaded dough into an oiled bowl, then

covered it with a clean dishcloth. She set it near the upper oven vents where it would stay warm while it rose.

"Your mom didn't teach Robbie to cook?" he asked as she washed her hands.

"Apparently not. Or if she did, it didn't take." Madeline looked at the timer, then picked up hot pads. The timer dinged. She took out the first pan of cookies and put in the second, then reset the timer.

"I wasn't around when Robbie was a kid. By the time I was aware of the world around me, he was off to college. So it was like being an only child. It would have been nice to have him closer to my age."

"I know what you mean. Ginger's nearly eight years younger than me."

"You took care of her."

He shrugged. "I complained a lot, but I knew my dad was already scrambling to take care of everything."

"He never remarried?"

"No. Some of it was he said he couldn't find anyone as great as my mom and some was probably because he had two kids and no free time."

"Did that make you more responsible than you wanted to be?" she asked, thinking his fussing over his sister probably wasn't new. She would bet he'd been there for Ginger since she was born.

"Don't make me into a saint," he told her. "I got into plenty of trouble in school."

"Like?"

"The usual stuff. Cutting class, being rowdy with my friends." He smiled at the memories. "I got cut from the junior varsity football team for tardies. I'm sure the plan was that I would be devastated and change my ways. But I found I liked hanging with my friends more than I liked playing."

Madeline grinned at him. "You do know we have retired NFL players in town. Don't let them hear you say that. They'll never recover."

"Yeah, I have my doubts about how much they'd care."

"So you'd survive if they didn't love your movies."

"I would."

She leaned against the counter. "How did you get started in movies?" she asked. "Did you audition a lot?"

He looked at her quizzically for a second, then held up both hands. "You didn't look? Online? You didn't use Google to look me up?" He lowered his arms. "I want to ask why, which is ridiculous. You're normal. I like that."

"Was I supposed to check you out online?" She'd thought about it, but somehow, after meeting him, it had felt as if doing that were an invasion of his privacy.

"No. You were supposed to do exactly what you did."

He rested his elbows on the counter and leaned toward her. "After my dad died, money was tight. I left college to take care of Ginger. I worked a couple of jobs to pay the bills. One of them was cleaning pools. A guy I worked for was a producer. We talked a few times and he offered me a chance to be in one of his movies."

"That was nice of him."

"It was. The pay was better than I was making at my other job." Jonny grinned. "He made me promise I would keep cleaning his pool, even after I was a movie star, which was supposed to be a joke. Anyway, I showed up at the studio. I had one line, which I delivered. Trust me, acting isn't rocket science. I had to stick around because they wanted to change the set or something. There was a call saying the guy who was supposed to be the sidekick broke his leg skiing."

Madeline winced. "That can't be good for anyone."

"It wasn't. Everyone was pissed. They wanted to keep doing the scene, so they asked me to stand in for him. Just read the lines so the star could have someone to talk to. I knew nothing about the business, but I figured it meant an extra couple of hours not cleaning pools, so I agreed. The next thing I knew, they were having me read more scenes. Two days later, I was hired as the replacement."

"And the rest is history?"

Jonny grinned. "Pretty much."

"Did you keep cleaning your friend's pool?"

"For a year. Then he cut me loose."

Madeline liked that he'd kept his word. She wondered how many other people, in his position, would have blown off the promise.

"Do you like acting?"

"It beats a real job." His humor faded. "I know what I do is about entertaining people. It's not saving lives or changing the world, but that's not an excuse to phone it in. I want to do my best. To be at work on time, knowing my lines. I want to be in shape and have whatever fighting skills I'm going to need for the current project."

"You take pride in your work."

"Yeah. Too hokey?"

She shook her head because saying "Exactly right" could complicate things. The pretty face had been appealing enough, she thought wryly. The actual man was even more of a temptation. A problem she didn't need and wasn't sure how to handle.

"Do you film all over the world?" she asked.

"On some movies. It's always strange to go into a foreign country and yet be a part of the movie. We bring in nearly everything. It's like a strange movie-set community."

"Do you get a chance to see the sights?"

"Sometimes. It depends on what we're filming and how big my role is. There have been movies where there's a subplot that doesn't include me and others where I'm in every scene."

"Are you recognized everywhere?"

He shrugged again. "Sometimes. It's strange to have people speaking a language I've never heard come up to me and start talking."

She checked the timer, then used a spatula to take cookies off the sheet. "I have a friend—Felicia. She's supersmart and knows everything. She talks about how despite how technology has changed us, we are, at heart, still primitive people. We react to fear the same way, only now the threats aren't a big tiger that's going to eat us. She says that it's important to know the most important person in the village. That being connected to the power means getting shelter and having enough to eat."

She put down the spatula. "The need to be close to that powerful person hasn't changed, but because we don't have a village in the same way, we've transferred our allegiance to celebrities. We want to be close to them, to know them, to be a part of their lives." She sighed. "I'm saying it all wrong."

"No, you're not. I get what you're saying. That happens to me a lot. People think they know me because they know my character. Or they tell me they know we could be good friends."

Or the women want to sleep with him, although she appreciated that he didn't bring up that one.

"But they don't know anything about me," he continued. "What they see on the screen isn't real. I'm not a hero. I'm just a guy."

"A good guy," she said before she could stop herself.

He smiled at her. "I'm keeping my dark side hidden until after the wedding."

She laughed. "Does the dark side have a cape? Because that would be really cool."

The rest of the afternoon passed quickly. Madeline checked in with Isabel, who teased her about being snowed in and promised to lock up Paper Moon. Madeline heated the lasagna for dinner and was pleased that her rolls turned out. Jonny opened a bottle of wine for them from his cellar. At about seven-thirty the power went out. They sat in the dark for twenty seconds, then the generator kicked in and the lights were restored.

After cleaning the kitchen, they took a plate of her cookies and headed for the media room.

"I'm very excited," she admitted as they walked down the hallway. "Do you have your awards on display?"

"No awards," he told her, leading the way through a double door and flipping on lights.

"I know you've won something," she insisted. "I read about it somewhere."

"Yeah, yeah. Whatever awards there are I keep in my manager's office. Annelise is a much better steward of those kinds of things."

She took in the large room. There was a big black leather sectional facing a huge television. While she couldn't see any speakers, she had a feeling Jonny owned a sound system that could make the house shake. Oddly enough, he also had a record player and a stack of old vinyl records on a small table in the corner.

Instead of artwork, he had framed movie posters on the wall. Not his, but posters from old movies from the thirties and forties. On the back wall were built-in shelves filled with hundreds of DVDs.

"Nice," she said as she set down the cookies and crossed to the collection. "What don't you have?"

"Nothing I was in."

"Really?"

He nodded. "I don't need to see what I did. I'm not

egotistical enough to have to watch myself. Besides, my movies are like cotton candy. They dissolve in water."

"You're not giving yourself enough credit. Your movies are a great escape for people. They have fun. They remember them and quote the lines."

"It's not Shakespeare."

"You do know that his work was considered trashy back in the day?"

Jonny raised an eyebrow. "Look at you, all sassy with the literary references."

"I know things."

"Yes, you do." He stepped closer. "It's interesting how we both make memories with what we do. Mine are fleeting, but what you do lasts a lifetime. Every bride remembers her wedding gown."

Madeline thought about how Ted had always tried to make her feel bad for changing jobs so many times. How she'd always felt embarrassed for not being sure about what she wanted to do with her life. Even now she sometimes wondered if she'd been wrong not to finish her degree.

Only she loved her job, loved being a part of Paper Moon. She loved that she was buying her way into the business. Although she didn't need Jonny's praise, it was kind of sweet to hear.

"You're really nice," she said impulsively. "I wouldn't have guessed that."

He laughed. "People describe me in a lot of ways, but nice isn't one of them."

"Ginger thinks you're nice."

"She's my sister. She has to."

"She doesn't and maybe it's because she knows you best."

He started toward her, then stopped a foot away. For several heartbeats his dark green eyes gazed at her, then he turned and pointed at the shelves.

"You get to pick tonight. Anything you want."

A movie they would be watching together? In the snowy quiet? She hoped for the six-hour A&E version of *Pride and Prejudice*, but settled on a movie from the 1950s called *Summertime*.

"Excellent choice," Jonny said, taking the DVD case from her. "Smart and sexy, with a strong female lead. Considering the time it was made, a single woman alone in Italy who goes on to have an affair with a married man was considered pretty dangerous stuff."

"How can you know the plot?"

"I've seen it. I've seen every movie here." He motioned to the hundreds of DVDs. "For me, it's research. Why did one story line work and not another? What technique are the actors using? What can I learn from them?"

"Do you ever just relax and watch the show?"

"Tonight I will."

She sat down while he loaded the DVD. When he joined her, she hoped he would settle close, but he kept a respectable distance between them. Darn and double darn.

Soon she was caught up in the beauty of Venice and the growing flirtation between Jane and Renato, and although she really enjoyed the movie, she couldn't seem to forget about the man sitting on the same couch. She was aware of his presence in the dim light, of how he sat so quietly. When they both laughed when Jane fell in the canal, she found herself wanting to shift a little closer. Just to be near him.

"Jane should have stayed," she said when the movie was finished. "They could have worked it out."

"He wasn't going to leave his wife, and she had a life back in Ohio."

"A sad, lonely life." They walked down the hall toward the kitchen. "You're right, though. I would never tell a friend to give up everything for a guy. Certainly not one who was married. But they were so good together. Maybe he'll go to Ohio and they'll live happily ever after."

He leaned in and kissed her on the forehead. "It's no surprise that you're a romantic."

Was he dismissing her? Was that a dismissive comment? The kiss was sadly fraternal, she thought. Here she was, snowed in with a sexy guy she had a mad crush on, and he thought of her as his baby sister. Or worse. He should have been swept away, yet there he stood. Completely unswept. Life wasn't the least bit fair.

"Thanks for the movie," she said as she put the leftover cookies into the elephant cookie jar. "Good night."

"Night."

She told herself not to hesitate. That if Jonny wanted to make his move, he was fit and agile and could certainly chase after her down the hall. Even though she walked as slowly as she could, nearly lingering at every step, he stayed in the kitchen. There was no plea for her to rip off her clothes, or let him rip off her clothes. In fact, there wasn't any conversation at all. Just the quiet of her footsteps on the carpet and the sad, lonely beating of her silly, girlish heart.

Madeline closed the guest room door behind her and crossed to the bed. She sat there for a second before drawing in a breath and vowing that when the wedding was over, she was going to have a long look at her romantic life—or lack thereof. She was going to figure out why she fell for guys who weren't available and what she could do to change. Because she didn't want to end up like Katherine Hepburn in *Summertime*—a middle-age spinster with no one to care about. She wanted what her parents had, what Robbie had had. She wanted love and marriage and kids. She wanted it all.

But until Ginger's wedding, she was going to have to deal with her crush and the knowledge that wanting wasn't the same as having. And wishing didn't make a man see you as the girl of his dreams.

Madeline stared at the bound pages in front of her. She hadn't known what to expect when Jonny had asked her to look over a script. She'd never seen one before.

"I thought it would be digital," she admitted, fingering the paper.

"I'm old school. I read books made of paper and I want my scripts the same way. I can make notes in the margin."

They were in the family room of his house, still snowed in. Although the storm had passed, the roads weren't close to cleared. Rosalind had texted earlier that morning to say most of downtown was closed. Madeline had agreed on keeping the store shut. They didn't have any appointments and it was close enough to Christmas that everyone would be focused on their holiday plans. Isabel was staying home, as well. No doubt kept there by her loving and concerned husband.

Which left Madeline staying with Jonny for yet another night. So far they'd had breakfast, then he'd gone to work out in his superfancy gym. While he'd offered to let her come along, she'd refused. She would have loved to watch him sweat, but didn't know how to say that without sounding like a ridiculous groupie. And having him watch her pant her way through a very beginner walking program on the treadmill was not her idea of a good time.

They'd had lunch and he'd asked if she wanted to look at a script he was considering.

"What's it about?" she asked.

"Read it and find out." He glanced away from her, then back. "I'd like to know what you think."

There was something in his tone. She couldn't define it exactly, but if she had to guess, she would say he was unsure. About the project?

"Okay, sure. I've never read a screenplay before."

"The formatting takes some getting used to. You can ignore the stage directions. Just read the dialogue. Pretend it's an audio book."

She nodded and settled on the sofa. Within a couple of pages, she was caught up in the story of Dean Woodley, a guy from the wrong side of town who was determined to make it to the top. Through a series of unexpected events, Dean found himself fostering three street kids who were desperate for connection and guidance, even as they stole from him and nearly got him arrested for drug dealing.

The story was gritty and funny and, when one of the boys was killed in a drive-by shooting, devastating. Madeline read until the end, when the two remaining boys graduated from high school and Dean won the girl. Then she went back to the beginning and read it all again. When she'd finished for the second time, she looked up to find several lamps on and Jonny watching her from the other end of the sofa.

"You're crying," he said as he handed her a tissue.

"Am I?" She wiped away her tears. "What time is it?"

"Nearly six."

"I read all afternoon? I'm sorry."

"Don't be. I asked you to read it. What did you think?"

She hugged the script close. "I loved it. I'm usually a fast reader, but it took me a while to get over all the stage directions, or whatever they're called. This is such a great story."

She thought about *Amish Revenge* and all the other movies he'd starred in. Each of those characters had been a variation on a theme. Dean Woodley was completely different. "Are you thinking of doing this?"

"I don't know. I want to. Annelise thinks it's a good idea but then she's always seen more in me than I do. It's not what my fans expect of me."

"That's not a bad thing." She put the screenplay on the coffee table. "I don't know how the business works and I don't think I could tell a good screenplay from a bad one. What I can say is this was compelling and interesting." She smiled. "I like that he gets the girl at the end."

"Of course you do. You sell wedding gowns. Happy endings matter to you."

"To you, too. Are you worried that it's not a Jonny Blaze movie if you don't kick some bad-guy butt?"

"Yes. I wouldn't in this one."

"I think people would be okay with that."

"Thank you," he said. "I appreciate your opinion."

"Why?" she asked, before she could stop herself.

"You have good taste. You're honest."

Couldn't she be sexy instead? She held in a sigh. She would accept that she was the golden retriever of women in his life and try to be happy with that.

"We need to think about dinner," she said. "Do you

remember which casserole I took out this morning? I think it was tamale pie. That's going to be great. There's enough salad left from last night, and cookies. Because it wouldn't be a good dinner without cookies."

She paused, waiting for Jonny to say something. Instead, he stared at her. She had no idea what he was thinking. It could have been anything from him silently counting the minutes until he could finally take her back to town to a deep desire for peanut butter cookies. What she didn't expect was for him to slide the few feet separating them, gather her in his arms and kiss her.

His mouth was warm and gentle, with the most delicious hint of wanting. At least, that was what it felt like from her end. Of course, she was so incredibly shocked that she could have been wrong about all of it.

Still, his lips on hers felt nice. Right. And his hands moving up and down her back were great, too. Madeline had no idea what was happening, but somehow that was okay. Because if a girl had to be confused, then having that happen in Jonny's arms was the best place for it to be.

She let her eyes sink closed and her body relax. She gave herself over to the feel of his mouth teasing hers. She wrapped her arms around his neck, leaned forward and surrendered to the heat building up inside of her.

When he brushed his tongue against her bottom lip,

she parted right away. He eased inside. At the first stroke of his tongue against hers, flames ignited all over her body. Even though she was sitting, her thighs began to tremble. Wanting grew. She thought about how alone they were and how incredibly comfortable the sofa was. She thought about the fact that it was practically Christmas and she hadn't bought herself a single thing. Could one magical night with this man be her gift from her to her?

He deepened the kiss. She tangled with him, liking the way they found a rhythm that set her blood to bubbling. He slipped one hand from her back to her side. From there it went up and up and—

He drew back. "I'm sorry."

She managed to blink.

He stood up and walked to the other side of the room. "Madeline, I'm sorry. I gave you my word. I promised nothing would happen. That you were safe here. It's just…" He swore under his breath.

She didn't catch the exact words, but she got the general idea. Far more interesting was the, um, *proof* that she hadn't been the only one affected by what they'd been doing.

She told herself to look away, that it was rude to stare at a man's erection. But she couldn't help herself. Because she liked him and knowing he liked her back was really cool. Plus, the bulge was impressive.

"You're not listening," he said.

She returned her attention to his face. And while it was a very nice face, the hard-on was far more intriguing right now.

"Madeline, this is serious. I said nothing would happen."

"Last night," she blurted. "You said nothing would happen last night. And it didn't." She had the chagrined heart to prove it.

"You're not mad?"

"Why would I be mad? Do women generally get mad when you make out with them? Because if they are mad, you're doing something wrong." From where she was sitting, he'd been doing everything right.

Something flashed in his eyes. She had no idea what it was, but hoped it was understanding. Or uncontrollable lust. The latter would be her first choice.

He took a step toward her, then paused. "I like you."

Words to make her quiver. "I like you, too."

"You're stuck here because of the storm. I don't want you to feel pressured. Or obligated. I don't want you to think this is some kind of movie scene."

Understanding dawned as she finally got what he'd

been unable to say, perhaps even understand himself on anything but the instinctual level. He was a famous movie star. Because of that, women did things, offered things, they never would in their normal life. They didn't want to be with *him*, they were interested in the star. He was simply a means to an end.

Because of that, he would never want to put anyone in the position of having to perform. Because that was expected of him.

She thought about all the people he'd loved and lost. His mother, his first girlfriend, his father. Then she tried to imagine what it would be like to be so famous that women he'd never met would desperately want to sleep with him so they could say they had. No wonder he was wary of getting involved. No wonder he was fiercely protective of his privacy.

He liked her. He'd said it. They were friends. He saw her as a person and knew she saw him the same way. Even more significant, he was protective of her.

The thoughts flashed through her mind in a single heartbeat, then she was moving toward him. When she stood in front of him, she took both his hands in hers and smiled at him.

"I think the movie thing is really great, and I'll admit when we first met I was totally starstruck."

He watched her without speaking.

"But that went away pretty fast," she continued. "I like how you care about your sister and that you flashed your butt at Eddie and Gladys."

One corner of his mouth turned up. "Did you really mean to put those in the same sentence?"

"No, but go with it." She looked into his eyes. "You helped me with Ted. You make toys for kids and you have terrible taste in wedding cakes. I don't feel trapped or pressured and I know this isn't a movie scene."

She wanted to mention the erection, but wasn't sure he would get how cool that was.

"I want you," he murmured.

Oh, my. She felt both weak and incredibly strong. Hunger burned, but also an unexpected tenderness.

"Then I think you should have me."

The smile returned. "Yeah?"

Before she could answer, he'd pulled her close and pressed his mouth to hers.

❧ ELEVEN ❧

MADELINE WOKE UP WITH A warm arm draped around her waist and the glow of a clock telling her it was 5:01. She stared at the small numbers as if studying them would convince her it had all really happened. She'd spent the night with Jonny.

A happy scream built up inside. She did her best to suppress it. The man was probably exhausted. She was, too, but also excited and nervous and confused.

Being with him had been magical. He'd been a caring, considerate lover with more concern for her pleasure than his own. They'd made love, then eaten dinner, then had made love again. When they'd finished the second time, he'd pulled her close, as if he'd expected she would stay in his bed. So she had. Which explained why she found herself there at 5:02 in the morning.

He shifted in his sleep, releasing her. She listened to the sound of his steady breathing before sitting up and reaching for the robe she was borrowing. She pulled it on as she walked out of the master and down the hall to the guest room. Once there, she closed the door and turned on a light.

Her hands were shaking, she thought as she stood there, trying to catch her breath. *She* was shaking. Nerves, maybe. A reaction to what had happened. While she wasn't a virgin, she hadn't bounced in and out of bed with a lot of guys. Her relationship with Jonny was complicated. Her fan-girl feelings had given way to genuine emotions. Now they'd become lovers and she wasn't sure what that meant to her heart. Being around him was easy—too easy. Falling for him would be dangerous. Now that they'd been intimate, she was going to have to start worrying about her heart.

But how was she supposed to resist him? It had been difficult enough before, when she hadn't known what a temptation he was. But now, she not only had to deal with the fact that he was funny and sweet and caring, she also had to accept that the man was practically a god in bed.

The way he'd touched her, the way he'd kissed every inch of her, over and over again. How he'd caressed her breasts and the rest of her. The feeling of him being inside of her, holding her, breathing her name.

She crossed to the guest bed and sat down. Her mind whirled and images from their night together overwhelmed her. She felt foolish and hopeful and a thousand other emotions she couldn't begin to name.

Her cell phone chirped. Who would be contacting her at five in the morning? She picked it up and saw the city alert system had sent out a text saying the roads were being plowed. She scrolled through the list and saw the road to Jonny's ranch had been plowed around midnight. She was free to leave. Only she didn't really want to, and even if she did, she didn't have a car.

Knowing she had to keep busy or go crazy, she took a quick shower, then dressed. It was all of 5:25. Now what?

Her heart and her body wanted her to crawl back in bed with Jonny and go for round three. Her head was more wary. Had it been just a one-night thing? Were they now in a relationship? What happened when she stopped being able to hide behind the star-power excuse and had to face the fact that the tingles and zings were all about the man?

She was her mother's daughter and Loretta often talked about the lightning bolt that meant falling in love. Tingles and zips were not the same thing…right?

Madeline flopped back on the bed and closed her eyes. Now what? What was she supposed to say over breakfast?

On the ride back to town? They still had a wedding to plan together. She was pretty sure she could keep it together if she just had a couple of hours to herself.

She sat up and reached for her phone. There was only one person she knew who would be awake at this hour. Awake and willing to help out a friend. She dialed.

"Hello?" Shelby Gilmore said a second later.

"It's Madeline."

Shelby laughed. "What on earth are you doing up at five-thirty in the morning?"

"It's a long story. I need a ride home."

There was a pause. "From somewhere other than home?"

"Uh-huh."

"Where would that be?"

Madeline bit on her lower lip.

"If you don't tell me, it's going to make picking you up more challenging. I'm sorry to say my telepathic directional abilities are not what they should be."

An excellent point. Madeline sighed. "The old Konopka Ranch," she said quickly, then braced herself for the reaction.

"The old what?"

Crap. Shelby hadn't lived in Fool's Gold very long. She would only know it as… "I'm at Jonny Blaze's house."

Silence.

"I know what you're thinking," she said quickly. "I know, believe me. It's just… I don't know. I need to get home. Please."

"It's fine. Stop talking. You don't have to explain." Shelby's voice was gentle. "I'm picking up my keys as we speak. I'll be there in about thirty minutes."

"Thank you."

Madeline hung up, then collected her things. There wasn't much beyond the clothes she was wearing and her handbag. She retreated to the kitchen where she spent fifteen minutes writing a note. On her third try, she knew she wasn't going to possibly get it right, mostly because she didn't know what to say. In the end, she settled on *"The roads are open and I caught a ride back to town. Thanks for everything."*

She wanted to say more. She wanted to mention how happy he'd made her as he'd held her in his arms. How his combination of gentleness and passion had helped her feel treasured and special. That usually the first time she was with a guy she couldn't slip over the edge, but with him she'd been able to relax. That she'd liked how he'd held her after, and that they'd laughed over dinner and, well, everything.

Tingles, she told herself firmly. She was experiencing

tingles. Not love. She refused to fall for a guy who was so afraid of losing yet again that he never offered his heart.

She walked to the living room and watched out the front window. When a familiar Subaru pulled into the circular driveway, Madeline let herself out of the house.

She hurried to the car and got in. Shelby, a petite blonde with the delicate bone structure of a fairy princess, looked at her.

"Should I be worried?" her friend asked.

"Not yet."

Shelby nodded and drove around to the main road. When they reached it, she turned left, back toward town.

"You know I love you," Shelby said a couple of minutes later.

"You closed the bakery and drove out here at five-thirty in the morning without asking why," Madeline said. "Yes, I know you love me."

"You like the guy?"

"I'm not sure."

That earned her an eye roll.

Madeline sighed. "Yes, I like him."

"Thank you for admitting it. You're not the type to sleep with someone without liking him first."

"How do you know we slept together?"

Shelby groaned. "Seriously? You expect an answer to that?"

Madeline sighed again. "I'm confused."

"You're running."

"No. I'm getting back to town so I can…" As she refused to sigh a third time in ten seconds, she was forced to hang her head. "I ran."

"You ran out on someone you care about. After being snowed in at his house. At Christmastime."

"I'm a horrible person."

"I still love you. But you might want to be thinking of a way to explain it all. If you want to see him again."

Oh, no! Madeline hadn't thought that part through. For a second she considered asking Shelby to turn around, but changed her mind. She needed to think. She needed a little space and she really needed to change her clothes.

"I'll send him a text," she said.

"That's romantic."

"Hey, what about being on my side?"

Shelby drove into Fool's Gold. "You don't get to have attitude this morning, missy. I closed the bakery and drove up a mountain for you. Remember that."

Madeline smiled at her. "I will. Forever."

Jonny read the text again. It was simple and to the point. I freaked. I'm sorry. Can we talk later?

He supposed he could be pissed, but in truth, he appreciated the honesty in the message. Last night had been unexpected—for both of them.

He'd already showered and had breakfast. Now he wandered through his house and tried to figure out how it could feel so empty. Madeline had been with him less than forty-eight hours. There was no way she could have had such an impact on him or the place. Yet here he was, walking around as if he were a lost puppy.

He checked his email, then flipped through the script Madeline had read the previous day. It would be a departure for him. Something no one expected. He told himself that stretching was good, and if he failed, he could always make *Amish Revenge 3*.

By noon he couldn't stand his own company. He drove into town and parked by Paper Moon. He walked toward the store, reached the door, then turned away. Madeline was working. They had nothing to say to each other that couldn't wait. He wasn't some sixteen-year-old kid after his first date.

All of which sounded logical, but didn't take away the need to see her. Finally he turned in the other direction and began walking.

Snow was piled up high everywhere. The streets and sidewalks were cleared and the temperature had climbed high enough that the sound of music, car engines and conversation was accompanied by the steady drip-drip of melting snow. Figured a blizzard would be followed by a warm-up.

He headed for the lake, then walked by Morgan's Books before stopping at Plants for the Planet. Knowing he was fifteen kinds of an idiot, he walked inside.

Ten minutes later he was going back the way he came, but this time with two dozen red roses. Talk about a cliché. Worse, he knew he was grinning like a fool and he couldn't stop. Nor did he seem to care.

He pulled open the door to Paper Moon. Madeline was with a client and the first thing he heard was the sound of her laughter. She and a bride were trying on different shoes with a fitted dress that flared out at the bottom. The bride, a pretty brunette, teetered in four-inch heels while Madeline offered her arm for support.

"I want to be taller," the bride said with a laugh.

Madeline grinned. "I get that, but how much do you want to be able to walk?"

"You're saying I have to pick?"

"It's that or move the wedding to Happily, Inc., and have the Cleopatra wedding where you're carried in on a palanquin."

"A what?"

"The seat with the four guys carrying it on poles." Madeline dimpled. "Sometimes it's a crossword clue."

The bride wobbled and started to go down. Jonny rushed for her and caught her just as she slipped. He was careful to keep hold of the roses with his other arm.

Both Madeline and the bride stared at him.

"Wow," the bride said. "You look a lot like some actor... I can't think of his name."

Jonny winked. "I get that all the time." He helped the other woman back on her feet. "Mind if I steal Madeline for a second?"

"Go ahead. I'm going to stand here and will myself to grow two inches taller."

Madeline hesitated, then nodded. "I'll be right back."

"Take your time. I'm going to try on all the shoes again and pick my favorites."

Madeline looked at him. "Give me one second."

She hurried into the room that held the bridesmaids' dresses, then returned with a straight-back chair. She set it next to the other woman.

"Hang on to this. I don't want you falling."

"You're so sweet. Thank you."

Madeline smiled at her, then turned to him. "My office?" she asked.

He followed her down the hallway. They stepped into

her office. He closed the door and faced her, even as he realized he had no idea what he was going to say. Not that it mattered because, at that moment, speaking was highly overrated.

He put the roses on her desk and pulled her close, then kissed her. He was relieved when her arms came around him and she hung on as if she had no plans to let go. His mouth settled on hers and he felt the familiar heat and desire pouring through him.

There was something about being with Madeline, he thought, his blood pooling in his groin and his mind shifting from why he was here to what they could do on her desk. Some sexy combination of how she turned him on and how he liked being with her, regardless of what they were doing.

But this was her office and she had a client waiting, so he reluctantly drew back.

"I'm sorry," she said quickly, her blue eyes searching his face. "For what happened this morning."

"You freaked," he murmured, remembering her text.

"Yes. I woke up and we were naked and I didn't know what to think. Being with you was great." She bit her lower lip. "But confusing."

Because she'd been scared, he thought, her actions suddenly clear. They were friends and she was helping him with his sister's wedding. But there hadn't been any definition of what they meant to each other. They weren't dating, so this wasn't the next logical step.

"I'm not seeing anyone else," he told her firmly. "I'd like to be seeing you."

Her mouth curved into a smile and color stained her cheeks. She looked at him as if he'd just defeated an entire galaxy of invaders.

"Really?"

He kissed her again. "Yes, really."

"I'd like that, too," she whispered.

His chest tightened a little. It had been a long time since having someone want to be with him had mattered. Since he'd cared this much. He liked knowing that part of his heart wasn't completely dead.

"I brought you roses," he said, motioning to the flowers. "I went traditional."

She picked them up and breathed in the scent. "They're beautiful. Thank you." Her expression turned wistful. "I'd love to talk but I have to get these in water and I have a client."

"I know. I'll see you later?"

"Yes, please."

He started for the door, then turned back. "We're dating. Exclusively."

The smile returned. "I got that."

"I'm confirming. I don't want some tourist coming in here and sweeping you off your feet."

"I don't get a lot single guys coming into the store."

"That's not the only reason I worry."

She sighed. "You make it very hard to resist you."

"Good."

He walked out of Paper Moon. The sun was out, the snow a brilliant white. Everywhere he looked, there were Christmas decorations and happy people. Some called out greetings. He returned them with an easy smile. Today was going to be a great day.

Madeline raised her glass of iced tea. "We salute you," she said with a laugh.

Noelle giggled as everyone toasted her victory in the annual holiday window display contest. "We really worked it," she admitted. "Gabriel and I have been planning the windows since August. Josh gave me a run but we hung on."

Every year the businesses in town competed for the best holiday decorations. Well, not all the businesses. Madeline and Isabel had discussed joining the competition, but then had agreed neither of them were all that interested. Noelle and Josh were locked in a fierce competition and getting between those two would require way too much effort.

Instead, Paper Moon went for quiet, seasonal lighting and a couple of glittery snowflakes. Their customers seemed happy, the season was celebrated and no one was caught in the competition crossfire.

Bailey put down her glass. "I had no idea you were so competitive. It doesn't show at all."

Noelle sighed. "I'm not usually. There's just something about the window display contest that gets me going. Maybe because it's only at Christmas and I have the Christmas store in town."

Taryn looked at her. "I think you're hiding a killer instinct. You need to channel it into something safe or we'll all be in trouble." She raised her eyebrows. "I know. Isabel is having triplets. You could compete with that."

Noelle winced and held up both hands. "No, thank you. I surrender. Isabel wins. One at a time is plenty for me."

Isabel touched her rapidly growing belly. "I'm not sure this is a victory so much as an endurance sport. I'm torn between counting the days until I'm no longer pregnant and terrified of what life is going to be like with triplets."

Madeline knew that Isabel's mother and mother-in-law would be there 24/7, if that was what she and her husband wanted, but she also understood her friend's dilemma. Three babies at the same time? When was she supposed to sleep?

Shelby leaned close. "All this talk of babies is making me want to insist on bottled water. Something is going on with the birth rate in this town."

Madeline chuckled. "You know it's not in the water, right? I mean, do we have to have another talk about the birds and bees?"

"Very funny." Shelby looked at Madeline's phone. "Oh, look. You just got another text."

Madeline felt herself blush. She'd left her phone on the table, but had turned off the sound. Silly, really, but Jonny texted her a dozen times a day. Fun little messages that he was thinking of her or telling her about how negotiations were going on the Dean Woodley project. It was day two of dating Jonny Blaze and she had to say that, so far, it was pretty terrific.

Last night they'd gone out to dinner and then he'd stayed at her place. It had been magical. Now she glanced around the table to see if anyone was paying attention.

"No one knows," Shelby said quietly. "I haven't said anything."

Madeline saw that Shelby was right. Everyone else was

talking and no one had noticed the text or her friend's teasing comments.

"I'm just not ready to go public," Madeline admitted. "I don't know what people are going to say."

"They'll be happy for you."

She nodded, but on the inside she was wondering if they would all be questioning what he saw in her. She wasn't famous or beautiful or exotic. She was an ordinary woman living in a small town.

Larissa hurried into the restaurant and joined them. "Sorry I'm late," she said, plopping down next to Taryn.

Taryn looked at her. "Let me guess. You were doing something for Jack." She turned her attention to the table. "I love that Jack has found his career one true love in coaching, but to hear that one talk, he's saving the world."

"Starting a football program at Cal U Fool's Gold is a big deal," Larissa said, "but that's not why I'm late." She reached into her large tote and pulled out postcards. "I was picking up these."

She handed one to Taryn first, then passed the rest of them around the table.

Madeline saw it was a "save the date" card for the surprise anniversary party Larissa was throwing for her husband. "Valentine's Day 2016," she read aloud.

"What day of the week is that?" Shelby asked.

"Sunday," Larissa and Madeline said together.

Shelby shook her head. "I guess Larissa would know that because it's the day of her big party. How do *you* know it?" Her expression brightened. "Oh, it's a wedding gown thing, right?"

"Uh-huh. Valentine's Day is very popular with brides. I know the date of every significant holiday in 2016, not to mention every Saturday from May through September."

"All the women in my life are impressive," Taryn said with a happy sigh. She turned to Larissa. "Big party?"

Larissa grinned. "Only the best for Jack."

"Dear God, you're renting out some stadium, aren't you?" Taryn leaned over and hugged her friend. "If it makes you happy, then it makes me happy, too."

Madeline watched everyone chat with Larissa. Talk turned to other weddings and upcoming events. Taryn looked at Madeline.

"So," she said. "About Jonny Blaze."

Madeline froze. How had Taryn figured it out so quickly? She knew Shelby hadn't said anything, which meant what? They'd been spotted together? Madeline had the obviously "I've been having amazing sex with a fantastic guy" glow?

"He got in touch with me this morning," Taryn continued. "He said he's willing to donate a bunch of toys to the drive, but they aren't ready and that you would know about them. That they need to be painted first?"

Madeline's relief was immediately followed by guilt and panic. In all the excitement of taking things to the next level with Jonny, she'd totally forgotten about the toys. So while the world didn't know they were having sex, she was a horrible person for not following through on Christmas gifts for needy kids.

"I forgot," she said, pressing a hand to her chest. "Oh, no. Children aren't going to have toys because of me."

Taryn pulled her phone out of her handbag and entered her password. "Don't be silly. No one's Christmas is going to be ruined. We'll organize a paint party. Let me look at the Sprouts' calendar to see what's what. We have an activity day planned already. It's only a couple of days before the end of the drive, but it can't take that long for paint to dry."

Shelby was already texting. "Let me check with Destiny and Starr. I'm sure they can help."

Bailey was on her phone, as well. "I'm sending myself a note. Taryn, once you get the date and time nailed down, I'll put out the word in town. Madeline, let me know how many more people you're going to want. Eventually, we'll hit the point of diminishing returns."

Madeline swallowed against the tightness in her throat. Of course, she thought with relief. She wasn't in this alone. There was no way her town was going to let children be disappointed on Christmas. She could screw up and someone would always be around to help her figure out a way to make it better. She still had to deal with the fact that she'd forgotten about the toys, but that was for later. Right now the more important problem had been fixed.

She promised to talk to Jonny about the work area where the toys were so they could decide how many people would be helpful and at what point there would be too many hands to be efficient. Conversation shifted to more personal topics. Isabel teased Taryn about what designer something Angel would be getting her this year while Noelle and Bailey discussed the best brunch casserole for post-present-opening Christmas morning.

After lunch, Shelby walked out with Madeline.

"You okay?" her friend asked as they crossed the street.

"Still feeling horrible about forgetting the toys."

"You know the problem's going to be fixed, right? You aren't the Grinch."

"I was so caught up in the guy that I let something important go."

Shelby waited until they were on the sidewalk before facing her. "Stop beating yourself up. Honestly, when was the last time you were this crazy about someone?"

"I can't remember."

"Exactly. So enjoy every minute of it. It's the holidays. You're allowed to have a good time. The toys will get painted, children will be happy and you still get to have hot monkey sex with you-know-who."

Madeline hugged her friend. "You're a very nice person."

"So I've been told."

They started walking again. Madeline unfastened her jacket. "It's really warm. I can't believe that two days ago we were in the middle of a blizzard. It has to be at least fifty degrees."

"It's very strange weather," Shelby said. "The weather guy said it was going to stay warm through tomorrow and then we get sideswiped by a polar vortex. So there's still a possibility of a white Christmas."

"I hope we get at least a light dusting. The kids always love that." Not to mention how beautiful Ginger's wedding would be.

They reached Paper Moon. Shelby smiled. "You okay?

I don't have to worry that you'll be beating yourself up all afternoon?"

"I have a couple of appointments, so I won't have time for major guilt. But I will probably still have a little self-loathing."

"As long as it doesn't go on too long. You're a good person, too. It's okay to mess up once in a while. Everyone still loves you."

"Thanks."

Madeline went into the store and walked to her office. After hanging up her coat, she turned to her desk. Sitting next to her keyboard was a small gold box. She recognized it as coming from the local candy store.

Inside was one perfect, dark chocolate truffle. Her favorite kind. There wasn't a note, but she knew who had delivered the sweet to her. Because Jonny was nothing if not thoughtful.

Talk about hard to resist, she thought as she put the truffle in her desk drawer. How was she supposed to keep things light when every time she was around him, he got better and better?

If only… If only he wanted something more. An impossible dream, she told herself firmly. Even if this was Christmas, and a time for miracles.

❧ TWELVE ❧

"YOU KNOW YOU DON'T HAVE to be here, right?" Madeline asked in a low voice.

Jonny grinned at her. "I can't help myself. It's better than reality television."

"It's a meeting about the Live Nativity. How is that compelling?"

"I want to hear the discussion on which animals will be allowed. Plus, who knows what Eddie and Gladys will get up to."

"You so need to get back to work."

He winked. "You'll miss me when I'm gone."

That was truer than he knew, she thought, determined to stay positive and hopeful.

Eddie and Gladys walked into the conference room. They glanced around, saw Jonny and walked over to sit across from him.

"It's too hot outside," Gladys said, slipping out of her coat. "It's nearly Christmas. The snow's melting."

"It's supposed to get cold again soon," Madeline told her.

"I hope you're right. Seasons exist for a reason."

"Don't mind her," Eddie said. "She's having a personal summer moment."

Madeline wasn't sure what to say to that and she couldn't begin to imagine what Jonny must be thinking. But he'd been the one who had wanted to stay, so it served him right.

"Nice shirts," Jonny said.

Madeline saw the two old ladies were in their finest bowling shirts. The pink ones that had their team name embroidered in bright, tall letters.

"Hot Young Things," he read aloud. "Good marketing."

Eddie preened. "Aren't they nice? Gideon and his radio station sponsor us." Her expression turned sly. "Of course, if you were interested in sponsoring us instead, we could talk."

"They'd have to wrestle for the privilege," Gladys said flatly. "Naked."

"Naked would be very nice." Eddie sat across from Jonny. "Interested?"

"Let me think about it. The offer is tempting."

Eddie didn't look convinced. "You're messing with us, aren't you? You have no plans to wrestle naked."

"Or clothed," he admitted. "But planting the image is my holiday gift to you."

The old ladies looked at each other, then back at him. "It's a good one," Gladys admitted.

The meeting was called to order. Dr. Galloway put on her reading glasses and opened the folder in front of her.

"We're going to have both the potbellied pig and the fainting goat at the Live Nativity," she stated. "Unless the goat can't handle it. No one wants to see the poor animal so terrified it keeps fainting."

"I do," Eddie murmured.

"Is someone going to be on hand to take the goat home?" Madeline asked.

"May Stryker has volunteered to wrangle the goat." Dr. Galloway frowned. "Is that the right word? Wrangle? Or do you do something else with a goat?"

"In some parts of the world, they put them in stew," Gladys offered.

"I'm ignoring you," Dr. Galloway said without looking up from the papers she was studying.

"You always do."

Jonny leaned toward Madeline. "You gotta love this," he murmured. "It's classic."

"Somehow it's all going to bite you in the butt," she whispered back. "I can practically guarantee it."

Thirty minutes later all the last-minute details for the Live Nativity had been arranged. Jonny and Madeline walked outside. The temperature was still unseasonably warm. Snow melted everywhere and the streets were wet and muddy.

"When it freezes, the roads are going to be a mess," Madeline said.

Jonny leaned in and kissed her. "Then we'll make sure when that happens you're out at my place. You know, so you'll get stuck again."

"I like how you think."

Before she could say anything else, they were both distracted by the sound of spinning tires. She turned and saw that Eddie and Gladys were stuck in the muddy slush. Their big sedan sat with spinning tires.

Eddie rolled down the driver's-side window and waved them over.

"Jonny, you're going to have to push," she said. "Say when and I'll give her the gas."

Madeline fought against a feeling of dread. She just knew that somehow this wasn't going to end well.

"Be careful," she told Jonny.

He nodded and walked toward the old car. He checked each of the tires. As he bent low over the front driver's side tire, Eddie got out her cell phone and angled it so she could snap a picture.

"Seriously?" Madeline called. "You can't give it a rest?"

"I've seen his butt naked," Eddie yelled back. "It's worth a picture or two."

Madeline wasn't sure if Jonny was listening to the exchange or not. She supposed he was used to being ogled. He walked back to her and took off his jacket, then pointed at the car.

"Can you get her to focus? There's no way I can push her car free if she's not giving it some gas."

"I'll do my best."

She draped his jacket over her arm, then walked toward Eddie. "You have to pay attention."

"No, I don't. He's a hunky man."

"You're stuck and, unless you want to stay here, you need to help."

Eddie looked from her to Jonny, then sighed heavily. "All right. We do have our Christmas bowling league party to get to."

Gladys took her cell phone and Eddie waved at Jonny. Madeline stepped back.

"They're ready," she called.

Several people had gathered to watch. A couple of guys joined Jonny at the back of the car. They lined up to push the big sedan away from the muddy curb. Madeline took a step back, then another. Her foot slipped on a patch of slush just as Eddie hit the gas and the big sedan shot forward and veered sharply to the left. Madeline saw it coming and knew she had to get out of the way, but she was still busy falling.

"Stop the car!" Jonny yelled, lunging for her.

He grabbed, she tried to stay on her feet, but the car kept coming and then Jonny shoved her hard. She slipped and skidded before falling into a pile of wet snow. Her body registered the cold and damp, but she ignored that. She spun and saw Jonny lying partially under the huge sedan.

"No!" She scrambled toward him.

Eddie had already stopped the car and was opening her door. The guys who had been pushing were rushing to Jonny's side.

"I'm fine," he said as he started to slide out from under the car.

"You'll want to wait for the ambulance," one of the men said.

"Does he need CPR?" Gladys asked as she came around the front of the car.

Madeline reached him. "Are you okay?"

He nodded. "Nothing's broken." He started to stand up, then winced and swore.

"What is it?" Madeline demanded, terrified of what had happened to him. "Is it your back? Your legs? Are you bleeding?"

From several blocks away came the sound of a siren. Someone had called 9-1-1.

Jonny groaned. "It's not that bad. Seriously."

"Too late," she told him. "The cavalry is coming and you're simply going to have to deal with it."

The good news was the EMTs had agreed to transport Jonny to the hospital without sirens. This despite Eddie and Gladys offering to lead the way. Fortunately, Madeline had told them they'd done enough damage for one day. The two old ladies had retreated to their bowling holiday party, leaving Jonny to deal with the humiliation of being taken to the emergency room in front of half the town.

"I'm fine," he told Madeline for the fourth time since he'd come back from getting X-rays. He ignored the throbbing pain and the seeping blood that stained the towel he'd been given. "It's a couple of cuts and a sprain. Nothing more."

She didn't look convinced. "It looks awful."

His left hand was kind of beat up. There was a growing bruise, a couple of gashes that were going to need stitches and some swelling around his wrist. It also hurt like a sonofabitch, but he wasn't going to mention that. She was already worried enough.

"I shouldn't have slipped," she told him.

She sat in the single visitor's chair in the small treatment room. He was on the bed, although sitting up. He refused to lie down. That was too much like admitting defeat.

"Did you plan to slip?" he asked.

"No."

"Did you slip on purpose?"

"Of course not."

"Then it's not your fault. Blame the weather. Or the fact that I insisted on coming with you to the meeting."

"You're not blaming Eddie and Gladys."

"They feel bad enough."

The two old ladies had already called twice to check on him.

The doctor came in and pulled up a stool. "Gabriel Boylan," he said. "You're right-handed?"

Jonny held up his injured left hand and nodded. "Lucky, huh?"

"Better luck would have been not to get injured in the first place. Hey, Madeline."

Jonny looked between them.

"Gabriel is married to my friend Noelle. His brother owns a couple of local radio stations." She pressed her lips together as if concerned she'd been babbling. "Is he okay?"

Gabriel looked at Jonny. "Do I have your permission to discuss your medical condition in front of her?"

"Sure."

Gabriel typed on his tablet, then turned it so they could both see the X-rays. "No broken bones. You're banged up and bruised. It's gonna hurt over the next few days, but you'll be fine. We'll need to put in a couple of stitches to keep the cuts closed while they heal."

The doctor went on to give him instructions on how to care for his hand. They had a brief discussion on pain-killers and how long Jonny should use ice.

"I've done this sort of thing before," he said without thinking, then wished he hadn't. The last thing he wanted to do was talk about injuries on a movie shoot. His hand hurt more and more, and while he knew he was going to heal, he also understood it was going to get ugly before it started getting better.

"Stopped cars with your bare hands?" Gabriel asked before turning to Madeline. "Did you get hit by the car?"

"No. I was busy falling into the slush."

"Bump your head? Your hip? Your knee?"

She held up both hands as if to show they were fine. "I'm wet from the snow. I had a soft landing and am dealing with nothing more earth-shattering than guilt."

Gabriel turned to Jonny. "Okay. I'll be back to suture you up and then I'll write up the prescriptions. Take it easy for the next day or two. No more playing hero." He stood, then crossed to Madeline and patted her shoulder. "You stay out of trouble, too."

"I'll do my best."

He left the room.

Madeline turned to Jonny. "You were saving me. I just got that. You put yourself in danger so I wouldn't be hit by a car."

Tears filled her eyes.

He was a typical guy who didn't like tears on any woman, but especially not when it came to the one he was seeing. Not that he didn't appreciate she was worried about him, but tears? He was prepared to do nearly anything to stop the flow. Lucky for him, her cell phone rang again.

"You should get that," he told her.

"It's not going to make me forget what you did for me," she promised, then pushed the talk button on her phone. "Hello?"

He watched as she listened. Madeline frowned slightly, then shook her head. "I don't have room. Four dogs? I know it's only for a few days, but I'm working. I couldn't leave them home alone at my place and I don't think I could get back to walk them." She listened for a second, then flushed. "No. I'm not going to ask him. You do realize we're in the hospital emergency room, right? Yes, he was hit by a car." Another pause. "Eddie and Gladys. No, he's fine, it's just…"

She sighed. "There has to be someone who can take them. I'm happy to help, take a walking shift or something."

"What's going on?" he asked.

"Just a second," she told the caller, then lowered the phone.

"The Day of Giving is Saturday."

"Yet another Fool's Gold festival?" he asked.

"Yes. Local charities have vendor booths so they can explain about their programs. There's also a pet adoption. It's become really successful, so they bring in pets from shelters around the state. Several dogs are arriving and they need a place to stay until the event on Saturday."

Now her conversation made sense. "You're right," he told her. "No way you could handle four dogs at your place. It's not big enough and you have to be at Paper Moon."

"I know. I feel bad, though."

"They can stay with me."

She stared at him. "Excuse me? You're injured."

"I have a hurt hand, not a broken leg. I can deal with a couple of dogs." He thought about the big open area around the ranch. Talk about dog heaven.

"It's four. How would you hold the leash to walk them? It's too much."

"You could help."

He had a feeling that Madeline would be open to hanging out at his place regardless, but a little dog guilt wouldn't hurt. And if she was fussing over him while loving on some puppies, all the better. Because being around Madeline was the best part of his day and he wasn't above taking advantage of homeless dogs to encourage her to stay close.

"It's Christmas," he added for good measure. "Don't those poor dogs deserve a chance to be adopted?"

She eyed him suspiciously, then sighed. "Fine. But when you don't sleep because you're overwhelmed by too much canine, don't say I didn't warn you."

"I won't."

Despite what he'd promised Madeline, Jonny fully expected to feel there were too many dogs in the house. He hadn't had a pet since he'd been a kid and going from zero to four was going to be a lot. What he hadn't realized was that in addition to the dogs, the town would show up at his place.

After getting stitched up, he'd been ready to drive home. Madeline had insisted on taking him, but first they'd had to fill his prescriptions. By the time they got to his house, there were already three cars in the driveway. Two of them belonged to shelter volunteers, ready to drop off the dogs. The other one was owned by a woman he'd never met but who wanted to drop off cookies and a fruit salad.

"While you're recovering," she said, handing the food to Madeline, before getting back in her car. "Good luck."

"Thanks, Maeve," Madeline called.

"Who was that?" Jonny asked.

"Isabel's sister."

"Isabel from Paper Moon? How did she know I was hurt?"

Madeline's expression turned pitying. "Everyone knows, Jonny. And this is just the beginning."

She was right. He'd barely been introduced to his temporary dogs when Eddie and Gladys arrived. Both women rushed into the house and insisted on checking on his wounds. Eddie hugged him tight. She was thin and felt so small and frail. While she was talking smack and checking out his butt, she was larger than life, but like this, she seemed tiny and old.

"I'm sorry," she told him, her mouth trembling as tears filled her eyes. "I didn't mean to hurt you. I feel awful." She sniffed, then swallowed. "We're not going to show your butt on our show. It wouldn't be right."

He'd caught their cable show a couple of times and knew the naked butt contest was their favorite segment. He took one of Eddie's hands in his good one and shook his head.

"You are so showing my butt and I am going to win the contest. Do you hear me?"

"You're not mad?" Gladys asked.

"No. I'm not." What had happened had been an accident. He was more relieved that Madeline was okay than worried about himself.

"We're going to take the dogs for a walk," Eddie said. "It's the least we can do. I have experience. I have a little dog. Marilyn. After Marilyn Monroe. She's a Chiweenie."

"A what?"

"Dachshund and Chihuahua mix. She's very sweet. It's nice to have a companion. All right, let's get your dogs together."

Jonny wasn't sure about two septuagenarians walking four dogs, but before he could voice his concerns, three teenagers arrived. They explained they were there to help out and joined Eddie and Gladys in collecting the dogs and herding them outside.

Jonny looked around his family room. There were large dog beds and bags of dog food. He could see into the kitchen where Madeline was sorting through all the people food that had been dropped off. In addition to the traditional casseroles, there were plates of cookies, pies and cakes along with a couple of six packs of beer.

"Exhausted?" she asked cheerfully.

"Kind of."

She'd insisted he take a painkiller, so he wasn't hurting that much, but the stress of what he'd been through was catching up with him. He patted the sofa beside him. She left the kitchen and joined him.

"How are you?" he asked. "Still no aftereffects?"

"Not a single one. I told you, I didn't get hurt." She studied him. "You're really okay?"

"I swear." Especially with her close. He leaned in and kissed her.

The front door opened and Eddie and Gladys walked in. They had one of the dogs with them.

"She's done," Eddie announced. "The other dogs wanted to run, but this one did her business and was ready to come home."

Madeline got up and took the leash from the other women, then read the tag on the collar. "Her name is Raven."

Jonny looked at the black lab. She was thin with a bit of white on her muzzle and kind brown eyes. As she glanced around, she seemed both sad and tentative, as if not sure what would happen next.

He had paperwork on all four dogs. He opened the folder with his good hand.

"Raven is nearly eight. Her family couldn't keep her when they moved into an apartment and she's been in foster care for nearly six months."

Madeline's mouth twisted. "That's awful." She stroked Raven. "It's okay, little girl. We'll find you a forever home. That's what Saturday's about."

Raven's gaze was steady, but her tail didn't wag. After a couple of minutes, she walked over to one of the dog beds and laid down.

Eddie and Gladys promised to come by the next day to help with the dogs. Madeline walked them out to their car. By the time they'd left, the teenagers were back with the other dogs. The kids helped get dinner ready for the dogs. Jonny noticed that Raven hung back. When she didn't attack her bowl, one of the other dogs started toward it.

"Not so fast," he said, and swept up the bowl, then took it into the pantry. He returned to the kitchen and got Raven, then led her into the panty and shut the door.

The dog looked from him to the bowl, then back.

"It's okay," he told her. "Come on, Raven. You've got to be hungry. I'll sit right here."

He pulled up a step stool and sat down, then tapped the side of the metal dish. She took a step toward the food, then another. Finally she was close enough to start eating.

He sat quietly while she finished her meal. When she was done, he stroked her back and then her face. Her brown eyes didn't have any hope left.

"You lost everybody, huh," he said quietly. "They walked away and you don't know why."

He had no way of knowing the circumstances that

had caused the former owners to have to surrender their dog. They could have been devastated or not cared at all. Either way, Raven had lost her pack. She'd been sent to a strange place and probably spent her days waiting for her family to return.

She was meek and underweight. He wondered if the other dogs she'd been fostered with had eaten most of her food. He didn't think it would take much to push her away from her bowl.

"It's going to be okay," he told her.

She turned away, as if she understood but didn't believe. He supposed she had a point. How could he know what would happen at the adoption on Saturday?

"Sometimes you have to have faith," he told the dog, only to realize it wasn't something he had a lot of himself. His sister's words seemed to echo in the small space. Her claim that he was so terrified of losing that he wouldn't risk getting involved. That he held back because the alternative was to connect and then lose.

He patted Raven. Her tail gave a tentative wag, then stilled. As if the price of believing was just too high.

❧ THIRTEEN ❧

"I could have helped," Jonny grumbled from one of the bar stools by the island as Madeline finished loading the dishwasher.

"You don't own rubber gloves," she pointed out. "You can't get your bandage wet. Besides, it's only a few dishes."

What she didn't say was that she liked working in his kitchen. It was big and bright. Overhead lights illuminated every corner. The appliances were new and efficient. A girl could get used to a kitchen like this, she thought humorously.

The visual perks weren't bad, either. Jonny looked good, as always. A little rumpled. Before dinner she'd tried to get him to take another painkiller. He'd resisted, and now as she took in the lines around his mouth, she wondered if he was in pain. His hand wasn't broken, but it sure was beat up. And the cuts had to be hurting.

She rinsed her hands before drying them on a dish towel, then walked over to his prescription bottles and shook one of the pills onto her palm. She handed it to him.

"I don't—" he started.

She walked to the sink and filled a glass with water. "I don't want to hear it."

"But I don't—"

She set the glass in front of him and put her hands on her hips. "Don't even get me started. I can be shrill. Trust me, it's a side you don't want to see."

His smiled. "Yeah, I'm scared." He took the pill and swallowed it, then drank some water. "The bossy thing is kind of sexy."

"You like shrill? I'm surprised."

"You only threatened shrill. I never actually heard it." He stood. "Want to walk the dogs before we watch something?"

"Sure."

It was still warm out. Warm and muddy, she thought as they collected leashes. Just the sound was enough to get the dogs on their feet. All except Raven, who raised her head, but didn't get up.

"Come on, Raven," Jonny called, his tone coaxing. "We'll walk slow."

The older dog rose slowly, then started toward him.

"I feel bad for her," Madeline admitted. "The other dogs are friendly and interactive, which means they'll have an easier time getting adopted. I hope someone takes the time to see that Raven is basically a sweet girl."

"Me, too." Jonny rubbed the dog's back before attaching the leash to her collar.

They went outside.

Madeline insisted on taking the other three dogs while Jonny handled Raven. She didn't want him having to use his injured hand.

They started down the driveway, then turned by the first barn. The night was clear and the stars bright.

"Too bad you don't have a view of town," she said. "It would be pretty tonight."

"It would."

"If only we could hear them whispering about you."

He chuckled. "I doubt they're bothering to whisper."

"Did you tell your manager what happened?"

"No. Annelise would worry and there's no reason for her to. In a couple of days, I'll be good as new."

"You could have gotten out of the butt contest. Eddie was feeling really guilty."

"But I don't want to. You think I'm going to let those sports guys hog all the Fool's Gold glory? No way."

Which was an interesting attitude, she thought. Jonny valued his privacy. He'd moved all the way out here to find peace from his star status. Yet he was willing to let a couple of old ladies flash his butt on their cable access show.

She wasn't sure what that said about him. Obviously the town was sucking him in. She liked that he wanted to belong. But the competitive streak was interesting, too. And kind of sexy.

"Before you know it, you'll be volunteering to be the sacrifice at the Máa-zib festival."

"I don't know what that is."

"It's a festival that celebrates the first settlers in the area. Hundreds of years ago a group of Mayan women left their village and headed north. They settled here and created a matriarchal society. Every year, at the festival, a female warrior rides a horse. The horse dances and then they cut out the heart of the male sacrifice. Not literally."

"Good to know. And you're volunteering me for this? I thought you liked me."

"I do, but you're trying to fit in. This is me helping."

He laughed. "That kind of help I don't need."

"Chicken."

"I want to keep my heart beating in my chest and not on some female warrior's plate."

"They just cut it out. They don't eat it."

"Still."

They walked along the gravel path. The dogs stopped to do their business and sniff the ground. The night was still. Madeline felt a whisper of cold on her cheek. As she turned toward the sensation, she felt the temperature dropping.

"The cold front," she whispered. "It's right here."

They stood and let the chilly air wash over them. Raven moved closer to Jonny, as if concerned about the temperature. When they were both shivering, they turned back to the house.

"Does the spirit of the Máa-zib tribe live on?" he asked.

"Naturally. The kids collecting toys for the toy drive are part of the Future Warriors of the Máa-zib. It's a little like scouting, but with a Fool's Gold twist." She smiled at him. "The warriors are girls."

"Why do I know Eddie used to be one?"

Madeline laughed. "I'm sure she was."

"Were you?"

"Yes, I started as an Acorn and graduated when I was a Mighty Oak."

They reached the house. Jonny pushed open the front door, then waited for her to step inside. They unleashed the dogs. All four of them hurried inside. Raven walked the slowest, and when she was partway across the room, she turned back, as if checking to see if the humans were still there.

"A mighty oak?" Jonny asked.

"Acorns, Sprouts, Saplings, Sky-Reachers and Mighty Oaks. It was fun. I learned to tie knots and do crafts. My mom was a Grove Keeper."

His dark green gaze settled on her face. "And when you have a daughter?"

She felt the beginnings of a shiver, although it had nothing to do with temperature. Inside the house was plenty warm. "I hope she'll want to join the FWM and carry on the tradition."

"Will you be the Grove Keeper?"

"Probably. It's fun to be involved."

"I want to tell you I'll never get sucked into anything like that," he told her. "Yet here I am with a busted-up hand and four dogs that aren't mine."

"It's Fool's Gold Christmas magic."

"Are you an elf?"

The shivers became tingles and heated her from the inside out. "If you'd like me to be."

"I would. Very much." He moved closer to her. "Hmm,

I'm going to have a little trouble, though. What with my hand being bandaged."

"I think we can work around that."

She stepped into his embrace. His arms came around her as he kissed her. The feel of his lips on hers was magical. Arousing, delicious and unexpectedly tender. Just like the man himself.

Madeline woke sometime in the middle of the night. She wasn't sure what had disturbed her sleep. Beside her, Jonny was breathing deeply. He'd only resisted a little before taking a painkiller before bed. There'd been no sign of bleeding on the white bandage and he swore his hand barely hurt, so she didn't think he was the reason she'd awakened.

She got up and reached for the robe Jonny had lent her, then slipped it on and got out of bed. The night was still and dark. There were a couple of night-lights in the hall.

She walked to the living room to check on the dogs. They'd taken them out just before turning in around midnight, so she doubted they had to go again.

She turned on a small lamp and saw that they were all snug in their beds. There were… She looked around the living room. Three beds. Not only was Raven missing, but her bed was, too.

Madeline checked to see if the dog had dragged it behind the sofa, but there was no hint of the dog or her
bedding. She retraced her steps, not sure what to do next.
She supposed she should search the house before waking Jonny. With the cold front coming through, the dog
wouldn't do well outside for any length of time. Not that
she could have gotten out, but still.

She entered the bedroom. Something moved. She
turned and saw Raven curled up on her dog bed. The
plaid quilted bed had been placed on the floor next to
Jonny's side. The black lab raised her head and looked at
Madeline, as if wondering if she was going to get into
trouble.

Madeline crossed to her and knelt down, then gently
stroked the dog's head. It was only then that she realized there was a blanket draped across Raven. While it
was possible the dog could have dragged her own bed
to the master, there was no way she could cover herself.
Which meant sometime in the night, Jonny had gotten
up to check on Raven.

"Looks like you have an admirer," she whispered.

Raven's tail thumped against the thick fabric.

Madeline tucked the blanket more securely around the
dog, then returned to bed. As she settled next to Jonny,
he turned toward her and placed his arm around her.

"You okay?" he asked, his voice sleepy.

"Uh-huh. Shh. Close your eyes."

He drew her against him and sighed. She felt him relax as he drifted back to sleep. She lay in the dark, more awake than before. Her mind raced. The more she got to know Jonny, the more she liked him. How was she supposed to resist small acts of kindness, like looking after an old, lonely dog? And if she didn't resist, wasn't she in danger of losing her heart?

Madeline stared at the trays of food. There were appetizer samples and soup samples and salad samples along with multiple entrées and eight different desserts. A few of the items were what Ginger had suggested, but the rest, while probably delicious, were a little over the top.

"Three kinds of oyster on the half shell?" she asked, pointing. "Ginger doesn't like oysters."

"Other people do," Jonny said easily. "They go with the seafood bar. There will be shrimp and crab, along with different kinds of sushi."

Before she could scream at him, Ana Raquel, their catering expert, returned to the small tasting room.

"This is the last of it," the twentysomething chef said cheerfully. "I have to say, it was fun ordering with no regard for pricing. I swear, in my next life, I'm going to make sure I have that all the time."

Ana Raquel was a petite blonde with big hazel eyes and a happy, upbeat attitude. Madeline knew her socially, but had never worked with her before. All the brides who hired her loved her. Madeline figured her ability to look on the bright side would help when Jonny doubled the order and added fifty items two days before the reception.

Ana Raquel sat down across from them and opened her tablet. "I'll need to place the seafood order today. Some of it requires specialty items. Not for a sushi restaurant, but for me. My fish guy needs a few days to pull it all together. It's the holidays and all."

"Makes sense," Madeline murmured, even as she began texting Ginger. The message was simple. Do you like sushi and do you want it at your reception? She pushed the send button and waited.

"The open bar is easy," Ana Raquel continued. "We'll have all the usual suspects on hand, along with champagne. Wine will be served with dinner. Should we do a different wine with each course?"

"Yes," Jonny told her.

"No," Madeline said at the same time. She turned to him. "People have to drive back down the mountain. At night. They're going to be totally drunk. Unless you plan on putting up fifty people, you can't have that much alcohol."

"I've hired transportation."

"Excuse me?"

"Tour buses from Mitchell Adventure Tours. This is a quieter time for them and they have a couple of good-size vans and a big bus. There's also a service limo company in the area, although they're for the wedding party." He turned back to Ana Raquel. "Wine with every course."

Madeline thought about pounding her head against the desk, but before she could start, Ginger answered her text. Yuck and no.

"Well, that's certainly clear." She showed her phone to Jonny, then smiled at their chef. "No sushi."

"Really? I was looking forward to making it."

"The bride doesn't like it."

"Oh, well, that changes everything." She went through the dozen or so appetizer selections. They tasted and narrowed the choice down to four, keeping to their semitropical-Mexican theme.

"We won't have enough food," Jonny complained.

"You kind of will," Ana Raquel told him. "In fact, you're overfeeding your guests, but as long as the check clears, I'm okay with that."

They moved on to the soup course. Madeline had to

admit that Ana Raquel and her husband had outdone themselves. Each choice was better than the one before. The onion soup was deliciously savory, with a cheesy topping that melted in her mouth. The mushroom soup had an earthy, smoky finish. It was rich enough to make her wonder exactly how much cream they'd used, then told herself it didn't matter. She was only sampling and everyone knew that sampling didn't count—calorie-wise.

As they tasted salads, she noticed that Jonny still favored his injured hand. She knew he was due to start another movie in the next few weeks and hoped he would be healed by then.

Thinking about the movie reminded her that he would be leaving when he went off to do filming or whatever it was called in the business. That while he had a house in Fool's Gold, she wasn't sure he could be considered a permanent resident.

What would happen to them when he left? Would they still be together? For that matter, she wasn't sure how together they were now. They had agreed they were exclusively dating. They were planning Ginger's wedding, but when the holidays were over, did they keep seeing each other?

She supposed the most logical step would be to sit down and have a conversation. That was what most people did. With any other guy, she would have suggested that, but not with him. Mostly because she knew he would ask questions about her feelings and she wasn't willing to look inside enough to figure out the answers.

Next came the entrées. Madeline had to admit the filets were delicious, especially with the spicy salsa on the side. Ana Raquel said she could also easily do a fish option.

"Any vegetarians?" she asked. "Or vegans?"

"You sound almost eager," Madeline teased as she texted Ginger.

"I've never done much vegan cooking. When in doubt, add butter. But in vegan cooking, you can't. I think it would be a fun challenge."

"We define *fun* in different ways," Jonny told her. He leaned toward Madeline. "What does my sister say?"

They waited until the text came through.

No vegetarians or vegans, unless Jonny has given up meat. In which case he needs to see a doctor right away.

Madeline smiled. "Steak and fish are perfect."

"Salmon," Jonny said firmly. "Wild Alaskan salmon."

Ana Raquel sighed. "I am so in love with you. I can

do a creamy dill sauce that will have your guests whimpering."

"A sound we all want to hear," Jonny said with a chuckle.

They moved on to desserts. Madeline made a few moany noises of her own as she sampled decadent dark chocolate mousse, along with Ana Raquel's famous S'mores Bars. There were also two kinds of cake and a layered trifle.

"We're going to have wedding cake," Madeline reminded him. "I think one dessert is plenty."

Jonny shook his head. "It's dessert. Two options. The mousse and something else. No one eats wedding cake."

She thought about the cookies that would be the favor left at each place setting and abundance of food already ordered. Honestly, what did one more course matter?

"You pick," she said as she reached for her phone. Menu is final. No one will go home hungry.

Ginger texted back a happy face.

Ana Raquel wrote up the final menu. Jonny signed the paperwork and passed over his credit card. Once he'd signed, they walked back to their cars.

"Thanks for meeting me here," he told her.

"No problem, but I have to get back to the store. I have an appointment this afternoon with a new bride."

He nodded, then stepped close. After cupping her face in his good hand, he leaned in and kissed her.

"I'll see you later?" he asked.

"Yes. I'll be by after work."

"Not to help with the dogs," he said with a grin. "I still have teenagers showing up twice a day."

"That ends tomorrow." At the Day of Giving. The pet adoption was at the same time. "Oh, I have to be at work. Can you get all four dogs to the event yourself or should I—"

He pressed a finger against her mouth. "I can handle it. You're not responsible for me."

She winced. "Am I taking over?"

"You're taking care. There's a difference, and I like it. But you have a business to run. Let me deal with the dogs." He kissed her again, his mouth lingering in a way that made her think longingly of tangled sheets and this man telling her he wanted her.

"Tonight," he said.

"I'll be there."

Jonny drove all four dogs and their supplies to the pet adoption. Both it and the Day of Giving were at the convention center on the edge of town. Volunteers with the pet adoption had on cheerful red vests over their coats. While the temperature was cold enough, so far it hadn't snowed. He hoped that meant a big turnout for both events.

A woman checked him in and confirmed which dogs he'd brought with him. Teen volunteers reached for leashes.

Raven stood next to him, not leaning, but not moving away. He'd brought her in last and now looked at her.

She stared back, her dark brown eyes sad and knowing. She got it. She was being passed on to yet another caretaker. Her head lowered as she sighed and turned toward the teen who'd taken her leash.

Jonny thought about the logistics involved with being on location in a foreign country, of how a dog would tie him down. There were a dozen reasons to walk away.

"Wait," he said before the teen went inside. "Not her. I'm adopting Raven."

The teen looked from him to the dog. "Are you sure? She's kind of old. We have puppies inside. They'll be more active."

"I want her." He took Raven's leash. "Tell me what paperwork I need to fill out."

Jonny completed the forms, gave the organization a hefty donation, then took Raven's only possession in life—her plaid bed—to his SUV. After putting it in the back, he crouched down by the dog.

"We're together now," he told her, rubbing her ears. "I'm your forever family." He paused, wondering what else to tell her. "I'm in the movie business, so you're going to come with me on location. I hope you like it. The studio hires me an assistant when I'm filming. I'll make sure that whoever it is likes dogs. Oh, and we're going to Italy in a few weeks."

He wasn't sure how he was going to get Raven there. He didn't like the idea of putting her in a cargo hold on a commercial flight. But, then, he was Jonny Blaze. He'd never been much for demands, but maybe it was time to ask for a private jet to get him there. Then Raven could ride with him.

He chuckled as he imagined what Annelise would say when he asked her to arrange it with the studio. Knowing how much she loved animals, he would guess she would be in favor of getting Raven first-class treatment.

"Come on," he said as he rose. "Let's go to the store and get you what you're going to need."

Raven stepped close and, for one brief second, leaned against him. He petted her head before leading her to his SUV and helping her inside.

❧ FOURTEEN ❧

MADELINE WALKED INTO THE PET store and looked around. Jonny had texted her that he was keeping Raven and doing some shopping. She'd said she could take her lunch and had agreed to meet him there.

She found him in the dog food aisle, studying labels.

"Hey," he said when he saw her. He smiled and gave her a kiss, before handing her a can of dog food. "The lady at the adoption event said this was the closest to what Raven has been eating. That they get all their food donated by one of the big dog food companies. She said if I want to change what she's eating, that I need to do it slowly. Because, otherwise, her stomach will get upset."

"Makes sense."

He put a case of the food into a cart. There was already a large bag of dry food, along with several bowls.

"What do you know about a raw diet?" he asked.

"For dogs?"

"Yeah. I've heard it's really healthy. I wonder if I have to make it myself."

"Won't that be difficult when you're traveling?"

"I could hire a chef."

"For your dog?"

He frowned. "Too much?"

"Kind of."

He was adorable, she thought. Just as insane with Raven as he was with his sister. This wasn't a man who couldn't care, she thought wistfully. He showed his feelings, when he had them. Given the choice between showing and saying, she had to admit she would come down on the side of action. Rather than try to read anything into how he was with her, she turned her attention to the dog food.

"Why don't you keep Raven on her regular food for the next few weeks? She's going to have enough stress in her life, getting used to being in a new home and learning to trust that she's not going to be moved again. That will give you time to research the best diet for her."

"Good idea." He patted Raven. "Okay, we have food. She has a bed, but she's going to need a couple of others. For the family room and the media room. Maybe a new collar and leash. What do you think about a jacket? It's cold. And toys. We need lots of toys."

They walked through the store. Jonny picked out a couple of collars for Raven, along with a few leashes. He got a book on basic dog training.

"I want her to learn to go off-leash," he said. "There's a lot of land at the ranch. She could go running as much as she wanted."

Madeline watched him try several dog jackets on the lab. Raven stood patiently as Jonny checked out styles and colors. He settled on a warm plaid cape-jacket made out of a quilted fabric covered in a waterproof coating. He was unbelievably sweet, she thought. Gentle and patient when Raven was hesitant.

They got a couple of soft beds, including one with an orthopedic insert for aging bones. Next up was the toy aisle.

Raven was unimpressed with the toys that squeaked and she didn't show much interest in the balls, but when Jonny offered her a rope tied like a bone, her brown eyes brightened. She leaned forward and took it tentatively. As she held it in her mouth, her tail began to wag.

Jonny grinned and threw two more into the cart, along with a few balls and a couple of toys he could toss. They got rawhide bones, treats and then headed for the check-out counter. Along the way, they passed a display of doggie Christmas attire. He picked up a pair of antlers and fit them over Raven's head.

She looked at him, then sighed, as if saying, *Really? Is that necessary?* But left them in place.

Madeline felt her heart melt a little more with every passing minute. She reached into her handbag and pulled out a business card.

"Cameron McKenzie is a really good vet in town. You have an appointment for this afternoon."

Jonny took the card. "It's Saturday. Aren't they already booked?"

"Probably. I called and begged. I figured you'd want to get Raven checked out right away. Cameron is a friend. I've known his wife, Rina, forever."

"Thank you."

They moved forward in line. Jonny put the items on the counter while Madeline held on to Raven's leash. The dog continued to hold her rope bone and wear her antlers. When everything was paid for, they walked out to his SUV.

Jonny hugged her. "Thanks for helping me pick out everything and for the appointment. I want to make sure Raven's okay. I was going to call on Monday."

"You'll like Cameron. He's a good guy."

"You're coming over tonight?"

"Yes."

"Good." He kissed her. "I'm getting a tree."

"You have a Christmas tree."

"I have a fake tree a decorator put up. I'm getting a real tree. Want to help me decorate it?"

She nodded because her throat was too tight for her to speak. She patted Raven, then got in her car. After taking a breath, she told herself that throat lumps weren't the same as lightning and that she was perfectly safe on the Jonny Blaze front.

The only problem was that she was pretty sure she was lying.

"I can do it," Madeline protested, knowing it was already too late. Jonny had taken the train set from her trunk before she could stop him. "You do remember you have an injured hand, right?"

"I'm fine," he promised as he carried the box into the house.

It was dark already and chilly. Still no snow in the forecast, which meant she had no excuse not to get to work on time in the morning. Too bad, because being snowed in again sounded really, really nice.

Jonny had made good on his promise to get a real tree. Somehow he'd dragged the professionally decorated one into a corner of the dining room and had set up the new one in the family room. Lights were strung—quite the feat, considering he was working injured. There were boxes of ornaments stacked on the floor, along with a tree skirt still in the plastic wrapper.

"You've been busy," she said.

"We have. After we left the pet store, Raven and I bought the ornaments and lights, then went to the vet, then back to the Day of Giving with a final stop at the Christmas tree lot on our way out of town."

At the mention of the dog, Madeline turned to look for Raven. She was curled up on her new bed, looking sleepy and content, her rope bone tucked under one paw.

Madeline shrugged out of her coat and draped it across a chair, then stepped out of her boots. "What did Cameron say about Raven?"

"That she's a healthy eight-year-old lab. She's a little underweight. He would guess she hasn't been eating much either because she's depressed or because she's getting pushed from her food by other dogs. He also wants her to get plenty of exercise. That's the best way to keep her healthy."

As he spoke, he bent down and petted the dog. Raven's tail thumped on her bed.

"Then you have a plan," Madeline said, thinking the man and the dog looked really good together.

"I do. Want to help me decorate the tree?"

"You know it."

They discussed the color scheme they wanted. Jonny being Jonny had overbought and there were enough shiny, glittery decorations for three trees. They quickly settled on traditional red, green and gold decorations. She unpacked the boxes and he placed the ornaments on the tree.

About a half hour into their endeavors, she went into the kitchen to put a casserole into the oven, then changed into jeans and a sweatshirt that she'd brought with her. Jonny pulled champagne out of the refrigerator and, despite his injury, popped the cork.

"To celebrate my new committed relationship," he said, pouring them each a glass.

She knew exactly what he meant—that he'd adopted Raven. But for a second, she allowed herself to think he meant more. That he meant them.

She didn't know exactly when he'd transitioned from Jonny Blaze, Action Star, to the guy she was falling for. She'd started seeing him as a person almost right away. But the caring part—that had been coming on gradually.

She liked how much he loved his sister and how easily he fit into the town. She enjoyed hanging out with him. They never ran out of things to say to each other. They shared similar values and laughed at the same jokes. Being with him was…nice.

"I went back to the Day of Giving," he said when they'd each taken a sip. "There are a lot of charities in the area."

"Some come in from Sacramento and even San Francisco," she told him. "We get plenty of tourists this time of year and the organizations are hoping to attract attention. Did you find any that were interesting?"

He nodded. "I'm going to do some research, but I figure now that I'm living here, I should get involved."

"You could bring a lot of attention to any one of them."

He leaned against the counter. "Not my favorite part, but you're right." One corner of his mouth turned up. "I guess it's time to use my powers for good."

"As opposed to the evil you've been doing so far?" she asked, her voice teasing.

"Exactly." He nodded toward the family room. "Come on. Tell me about that train set you're allowing me to borrow. I want to hear the family history."

"Then I'll tell you. It belonged to my great-grandfather on my mother's side."

"I knew it would be something like that."

★ ★ ★

Jonny hadn't known what to expect for the painting party. Madeline had promised him lots of help and that the toys would all be painted in time to be given to the toy drive. He'd set up tables and chairs in the open area of the barn where they would hold Ginger's reception, then had put out the paints he'd bought, along with brushes.

Right on time, cars started pulling up in his driveway. Eddie and Gladys were the first to arrive. Both old ladies hugged him close. Eddie was near tears again as she asked about his hand.

"I'm doing great," he assured her. "Good as new."

She didn't look convinced and he hated to see her spunkiness brought low by a freak accident. Not knowing how else to restore her spirit, he decided to take one for the team and turned his back.

"Go ahead," he told them. "Pat my butt. You know you want to."

He thought they might hesitate, but he was wrong. Both old ladies immediately patted his butt. One of them lingered just a little too long and he was forced to step away.

As he turned back to them, they were shaking their heads.

"We should have gotten our cameras out," Gladys said.

"And filmed it." Eddie's expression turned sly. "Can we do that again, Jonny?"

"Not a chance. It was a one-time thing."

"Then we'll have to sneak up on you," Eddie said.

Jonny held in a grin. Order had been restored to the universe.

By ten-thirty, a dozen or so volunteers were hard at work. He watched his plain carved toys come to life with color. The cars and trucks were more interesting, the animals more real.

Madeline showed up with drinks and snacks, including three gallons of tea. Someone brought a docking station in the shape of a porcupine and hooked up their smartphone. Christmas carols filled the space, competing with conversation and laughter. He told Madeline what had happened with Eddie and Gladys. She laughed.

"I wish I'd been here to see it," she admitted. "They have style and you're a very good sport."

Faster than he would have thought possible, his toys were painted and laid out to dry.

"You doing okay?" Madeline asked as she came up to him and offered him a glass of tea. "Any regret over letting your work go?"

"None," he admitted. "The toys weren't doing any good sitting on a shelf. Better for them to be played with.

Plus, this inspires me to keep carving when I'm on set."
He bent down and scratched Raven. "I can't spend all
day petting you."

"Raven wants to know why not," Madeline teased.

She wore jeans and a red holiday sweatshirt with a
big wreath on the front. Her hair was pulled back into
a ponytail and she wasn't wearing makeup. She looked
good. Happy. Pretty. Sexy.

He was lucky to have found her. Something else he
had to thank Ginger for. Because if his sister hadn't been
getting married, he wouldn't have had the chance to get
to know Madeline.

He didn't know where things were going between
them. He wanted…

He pushed the thought away. No way he was going
to jinx what they had by talking about it.

"Have you heard from Ginger?" he asked.

"Uh-huh. She's going to be here day after tomorrow.
I can't wait to show her the dresses that have come in. I
think she's going to be thrilled with a couple of them.
She'll be a beautiful bride. I'm very excited."

Jonny glanced away. "I am, too."

"What?" she demanded. "What aren't you telling me?
What have you ordered?"

He shifted. "Nothing."

She put her hands on her hips. "It's something. What? You didn't actually arrange to fly in the Vienna Boys' Choir, did you?"

"No. They wouldn't come." He shrugged, not wanting to tell her about the special order that would arrive Thursday afternoon. "I upped the flower order. Just by a little."

"I'm not even surprised. Just don't do anything else, okay? We're down to the wire. We have the food and flowers done. The venue." She motioned to the barn. "It will be decorated later this week, so no late-night parties for you. I want the twinkle lights to stay firmly in place."

"Are you actually worried about me messing with the twinkle lights?"

"Not really." She glanced around. "I'm looking forward to seeing how it's going to look when it's done."

"Me, too. The guys doing the ice sculptures will be here tomorrow. The weather is going to cooperate and stay cold enough."

"You really are doing ice sculptures?"

"Do you have doubts?"

"I remember the giant wedding cake, so no. Okay, I have to go write up the toy inventory. You can stay here and supervise. Oh, and don't get too close to Eddie and

Gladys. Now that they've actually touched the promised land, they're going to be looking to do more."

"No good deed?" he asked.

"Not when it comes to them. They will haunt you."

"With you helping by pointing out where I am at any given moment."

"Pretty much," she said with a laugh.

Madeline hung up the last of the dresses. She'd had two appointments that afternoon, along with a few walk-ins. The latter had been more about dreaming than buying, but she didn't mind that. Many a later purchase had begun with a fun afternoon of playing dress-up.

Two of the samples arrived in sad condition. Flat and wrinkled. She would leave them hanging overnight, then steam them in the morning. Or maybe ask Rosalind to do it. Business was brisk and she had to learn to delegate.

After straightening several veils, she walked back to the main showroom. She looked at the tall ceilings and big mirrors. The lighting was good, but the walls needed a little sprucing. She had some ideas for colors. The wallpaper was in decent condition, but tired. She would love to take it down and replace it with paint. They could go with a faux finish. Cheaper than wallpaper and easier to update.

After the first of the year, she was going to set up a meeting with Isabel to talk about the wedding gown side of Paper Moon. Her business partner had been focused on the designer clothes business for a couple of years now. Madeline had placed the last sample order completely on her own. As she bought into the company, she was taking on more responsibility. She had a lot of plans and it was time to share them.

Her cell rang. She pulled it out of her pocket and smiled when she saw the familiar picture on her screen.

"Hi, Mom."

"Madeline, how are you? Your father and I were just talking about you, so I thought I'd call."

"I'm good. I sold two dresses today. Both to lovely brides."

"I can't wait to see the pictures. Are you ready for Christmas?"

"Yes. My shopping is done. I'm busy with Ginger's wedding. She comes in tomorrow. I'm excited for her to try on the dresses I chose. Are you and Dad all ready for the cruise?"

"We are."

"You're going to have a great time."

"I know, but I worry." Her mother paused. "Darling,

are you going to be all right by yourself? With us gone and Robbie not there, what will you do?"

"Mom, you're sweet, but let it go. We've talked about this. You and Dad are going to have so much fun. I'll be busy getting ready for Ginger's wedding. On Christmas Day, I have places to go. Seriously, relax. I'm all grown up. You did a good job raising me."

"I can't help it. We love you."

"I love you two, as well. Now relax and trust me to be okay."

They chatted a few more minutes, then hung up. Madeline went to her computer to check her email before heading home. As she sat behind her desk, she thought of her family and how much she enjoyed spending time with them. Within a second or two, her throat was tight and her eyes burned.

"Don't be silly," she told herself. "I'm fine. I have plenty to do."

Only this would be the first Christmas on her own. Maybe it was a rite of passage or something, but it also felt kind of lonely. Sure her parents would call, as would Robbie, but it wasn't going to be the same.

She sniffed, then sniffed again. In the battle, tears finally won. She sucked in a breath, trying to get control as she wiped her face.

"What's wrong?"

She looked up and saw Jonny standing in the doorway to her office, Raven at his side. The old dog had the rope bone in her mouth and Christmas antlers on her head.

"Why do you do that to your sweet dog?" she asked, hoping a bright, happy voice would keep him from noticing her ridiculous tears.

He was at her side in a second. He pulled her to her feet and wiped her face with his fingers.

"Tell me."

She stared into his green eyes. Funny how the more she got to know him, the less she noticed that he really was good-looking. Amazingly so. But somehow that didn't matter anymore. He was just Jonny now.

"Nothing happened," she admitted. "My mom called. She's worried about me being alone for the holidays. I told her I would be fine, which I will be. Then we talked and hung up and I started to cry. I don't know why."

"Yes, you do."

She tried to turn away, but he wouldn't let her.

"I've never been alone on Christmas," she admitted. "I know, I know. I'm acting like a baby. I have places to go. People to see. It's no big deal."

He smiled at her, then kissed her. "Have Christmas with me."

"What? No. You'll be with family."

"I'd like to be with you, too. There's going to be plenty of food. I'm having a chef brought in."

She laughed. "Of course you are. I'll be with friends."

"Then come over when you're done. Stay with me."

Stay with me and be my love and we will all the pleasures prove.

It was about the only poetry she'd ever committed to memory and she was pretty sure she didn't have it exactly right, but the point was clear.

She leaned into him, wrapping her arms around him. He held her close. She felt the heat of him, the safety of his embrace. These were the moments, she thought. She could believe everything was going to be fine. That she wouldn't get her heart broken and nothing bad was ever going to happen.

❧ FIFTEEN ❧

THE LARGE BOX WAS DELIVERED at nine in the morning. Madeline read the label twice. She knew she hadn't ordered a custom anything from that particular design house. The only person she knew who could afford those prices was Taryn, and her friend had already gotten married. Yet the box was addressed to her. Not the shop, but her.

She studied it for a couple of seconds before she realized that she knew exactly what was inside. Some ridiculously priced designer gown that Jonny had bought for his sister. Because he couldn't help himself.

"Rosalind, fill up the steamer," she called. "We've got a new dress in."

Although the box was larger than most, she knew the drill. Wedding gowns came in impossibly small packages. They had to be fluffed, then steamed into bride-ready perfection. The dresses she had set aside for Ginger were hanging in the largest dressing room. It would take a couple of hours to get this one in the same shape.

"Or longer," she murmured as she pulled the stunning gown out of the box.

She had to admit, he got the color right. Like her choices for the petite bride, he'd gone with a pale ivory. The warmer tone would complement Ginger's skin and hair color. But instead of a sleek, delicate silhouette, this gown was all about volume.

The tiny cap sleeves were layers of lace. The bodice was fitted, then the massive skirt billowed. Tiers of lace and silk fluttered to the floor. The train had to be at least eight feet long. The dress was heavy, and while the size was right for his sister, there was no way this gown could work. She would look like a child trying to wear an adult dress that overwhelmed her. No amount of tailoring could make this suit her delicate frame.

Madeline put the dress on a hanger, then hung it on a rack. She would give it an hour to shake out before starting the steaming process. She picked up the envelope containing the invoice, then nearly passed out when she saw the twenty-eight-thousand-dollar price.

"You really need to learn to say you love her," Madeline whispered, hoping Jonny had made sure the dress was returnable before he'd handed over his credit card.

Three hours later, Jonny and Ginger arrived right on time. Madeline smiled at Ginger.

"Are you excited?" she asked. "Or nervous?"

"Both," Ginger admitted with a laugh. "I can't believe how fast time is going. Oliver and I are so busy with our research. Thank you for all you're doing for us. There's no way we could get married without so much help."

Madeline hugged her. "It's been fun for me."

"Me, too," Jonny added. "Not that you were asking."

Ginger wrinkled her nose. "I've thanked you fourteen times already and you know it." She pressed her hands together. "I can't wait to try on the dresses. I love the pictures you sent." She held out a small tote bag. "I have my shoes and the underwear you told me to get."

Ginger started for the dressing rooms. "There are two dresses, right? We narrowed it down to that?"

Madeline looked at Jonny, who glanced around innocently. When he didn't say anything, she shook her head.

"You expect me to tell her?"

"What?"

"You have a third dress from your brother."

Ginger sighed. "What did you get?"

"Nothing. It's nothing. Another dress for you to try. It's beautiful. Tell her it's beautiful."

Having just spent two hours steaming it, Madeline was

intimately familiar with the designer gown. "It's lovely. Handmade. The lace is truly exquisite."

Ginger didn't look convinced. "But?"

"But you should try it on, along with the other two. I also have the maybe dresses from your last visit."

"Okay, then. I guess I should get ready." She headed for the dressing room.

Madeline started to go after her. Jonny grabbed her arm.

"You mad?"

She smiled. "No and not even surprised."

"Yeah?"

"You're consistent and adorable. You know that dress is never going to work, right? It will overwhelm her."

"But it's really pretty."

"Which translates to 'I can't possibly convince you so you'll have to see her in it to decide for yourself.'"

He kissed her. "I like that you're so smart."

"Sure you do."

Madeline went back to the dressing rooms and knocked.

"Come in," Ginger called.

Madeline entered and saw the other woman had changed into a nude strapless bra. She had on plain bikini panties and nothing else. The giant designer dress hung on a rack in the center of the room.

"It's huge," Ginger said with a moan.

"It takes a village and a really big crinoline slip."

Madeline got her into the puffy slip, then Rosalind came in and helped her get the dress onto Ginger. The second it settled on her body, she seemed to shrink.

"How many buttons are there?" Ginger asked.

"About five hundred."

The other woman laughed. "Only do the top two. Then please get my brother. Not only can't I walk, but no one should have to button me into this."

Madeline fastened a couple of buttons, then used clips to secure the rest of the back. She walked into the waiting area and motioned for Jonny to follow her.

"That bad?" he asked.

"I didn't say anything."

"You didn't have to. You have smug-face. That's your silent way of telling me I was wrong."

She turned toward him. "I don't have smug-face, and even if I did, you weren't wrong. You love her and you want her to have a beautiful dress. That's really sweet."

"Even if I didn't get the right one?"

Madeline smiled. "I'm really hoping you can return it."

She opened the door to the dressing room. Jonny took one look at his sister and sighed.

"That's awful," he admitted. "It's what? Too big?"

"Too much dress," Madeline told him. "Ginger is petite. She needs a gown that flatters her rather than overwhelms her. Go sit. She'll be out in a few minutes."

He retreated. She closed the door. Ginger stared at her.

"That was good," Jonny's sister said. "You totally handled the situation without making him feel bad."

"He did a sweet thing. He really loves you."

Ginger nodded slowly. "Yeah, he does. I'm very lucky. It's nice how you understand him."

Madeline got a little nervous about where the conversation was going, so she hurried over to help Ginger out of the big dress. Rosalind took it away while Madeline got Ginger into one of the dresses she'd ordered.

"This is my favorite," Madeline admitted. "If it looks as good as I hope it will, you're going to be stunning."

The dress was a beautiful creamy ivory lace covering a white silk sheath. The two-tone effect was subtle, but added a depth that was elegant. The neckline was a deep V, front and back. The dress was sleeveless and a modified trumpet style—fitting to midthigh before flaring out. Rather than being too puffy, the skirt draped, giving a nod to the modern style without overwhelming the wearer. In the back, the fabric pooled into a beautiful brush train.

"I love it," Ginger breathed as Madeline pulled up the zipper.

"There's more," Madeline told her, then reached for the beaded ribbon belt. It was the same creamy ivory as the lace, with hand-sewn beading on the front. She tied it in place, then smoothed the ends of the ribbon.

"If this is the one, when we get it fitted, we'll have the belt bow sewn into place. Then we'll cut it and add a couple of sturdy snaps to hold it closed for the day. The last thing you want to worry about is tying the bow over and over again."

Ginger blinked quickly. "Why am I crying?"

"You're supposed to cry when you find the right dress. Come on, let's go show your brother."

Madeline grabbed Ginger's shoes and followed her to the front of the store. Jonny came to his feet as his sister entered, then whistled.

"Sis, you're stunning."

"Isn't the dress beautiful?" Ginger asked, wiping away tears. "I love it."

Madeline got her up on the platform, then helped her into her shoes. Ginger turned and viewed herself from every angle. Madeline showed her how the dress could be bustled.

"We'll add extra loops and buttons," she said, holding

the train up. "From the back, it looks fantastic and the front lines are still perfect. You'll be comfortable, able to dance and look good in pictures."

She straightened and Ginger threw herself at her.

"Thank you," the other woman breathed. "This is perfect. I love this dress so much. I can't believe how much you're helping me."

Madeline hugged her back. "You're welcome. I'm having a great time."

Over Ginger's head, she saw Jonny watching her. When their eyes met, she felt a tug that went clear down to her heart. It had nothing to do with sexual attraction and everything to do with the man himself. The feelings were deep and overwhelming.

What she'd been experiencing hadn't been star power or even hanging out with a really great guy. It had been love. She'd fallen in love with him. Maybe the first day, maybe over time. However it had happened, she was in it now. Totally and completely in love with Jonny Blaze. What on earth was she supposed to do about that?

After Ginger's fitting, she and Jonny went off to finalize wedding plans. Madeline did her best to act normal, despite the voice screaming in her head. In love with Jonny Blaze? What had she been thinking? Only there hadn't been thinking. There'd been her heart, falling for a man she could never have. Not only was he totally famous and rich and who knew what else while she was the definition of ordinary, there was his whole fear of commitment. He couldn't even tell his sister he loved her. How on earth would he ever allow himself to care about anyone else? Madeline knew she was completely doomed. It was not a happy revelation only a few days before Christmas.

She walked through town on her way to lunch with her friends. The store windows were glowing with lights and holiday decorations. All around tourists shopped for last-minute gifts. People called out greetings to each other. Madeline did her best to smile and wave, all the while telling herself she was going to have to get it together before she got to Jo's. Otherwise, everyone would guess something was wrong.

When she reached the restaurant, she paused to draw in a few deep breaths. She could do this, she told herself. Act normal. She opened the door and walked in.

She was the last one to arrive. She saw that Shelby had saved her a seat. Bailey was there, along with Taryn and Felicia. Isabel had gone away with Ford for a few days before family festivities. Dellina saw her and grinned, then motioned her over.

"How's it going?" Dellina asked as she approached the

table. "Have you found a new career as a wedding planner or are you ready to pull your hair out?"

Before Madeline could answer, Dellina turned back to the table. "You all know that Madeline is planning Jonny Blaze's sister's wedding, right? I've been hearing from my vendors that you're doing a fantastic job, by the way. Everyone is loving the choices you've made." She paused. "Oh, God. I'm talking too much, aren't I? I had four lattes this morning. It's the caffeine. I'll be quiet now."

Everyone laughed. Madeline hugged her friend on the way to her seat. "I don't want your job," she said. "But planning one small wedding has been fun."

Patience, the owner of Brew-haha and apparently Dellina's enabler, nodded. "I'm sure it's been a good distraction, what with your family not coming for the holidays." She held up her hand. "You're a grown-up, you're fine and I know you had fifteen invitations for Christmas, but it's not the same."

Her words were kindly spoken and meant, Madeline thought. After all, she and Patience had known each other all their lives. Patience was a couple of years older, so they hadn't been in the same grade, but they'd grown up in this family-centric town and knew how that left a mark.

"It's nice to be busy," Madeline admitted.

"And hanging out with Jonny Blaze," Bailey added. "Do you have a crush on him? Isn't it fun? I had such a crush on Kenny."

"We knew," Taryn told her. "We all knew and were charmed by it. Now you're together and blissfully in love. Which is nice, but the crush was more interesting." She looked at Madeline and raised her eyebrows. "How's your celebrity crush going?"

"I'm over it," Madeline said, knowing it was the truth. "He's a regular guy now."

"Is that good or bad?" Shelby asked.

"Mostly good. It's nice to be able to talk to him without being starstruck. My sentences have gotten longer."

Everyone laughed. Madeline felt herself relax. No one knew that anything was different. As long as she thought about her friends and the holidays, anything but Jonny, she would be fine.

"The toys were a huge hit," Taryn said. "They were special and so well made. I hope he does more for next year. I plan to talk to him about that."

"He's a nice addition to the town," Bailey added. "He's friendly and participates. I was wondering if he would just keep to himself, but he doesn't. He gets involved. That's nice." She turned to Madeline. "How's his hand? I heard what happened and I know Eddie and Gladys feel awful."

"It's nearly healed."

"He adopted that dog," Larissa said. "You've gotta love a man who adopts a dog."

Conversation shifted to other people who had adopted pets and from there transitioned to who was doing what for the holidays. Madeline talked about the addition of the fainting goat and potbellied pig to the Live Nativity, and how special arrangements were being made in case the goat really was too scared to endure the event.

They placed their orders, and by the time her salad came, she'd relaxed enough to enjoy the company of her friends. But as she walked back to the store, her tension returned.

She was in love with Jonny. What on earth was she supposed to do with that information? He wasn't going to love her back. He couldn't. He'd told her a thousand times.

She should have protected her heart more carefully. She should have listened to her mother. Now she was trapped and she didn't know what to do to make it better. And she was going to have to do something. Or she would be facing something ten times bigger than the Ted debacle. And then where would she be?

Jonny spent the day with his sister. When Ginger left to drive back to San Francisco, he went home and got

Raven. The two of them hung around town until it was time for Paper Moon to close. Somewhere around five, it started to snow. A white Christmas, he thought. The kids would be happy. Plus, it would be a beautiful backdrop for Ginger's wedding.

He walked by the park and then up toward Madeline's store. He stopped to buy her fudge and then did a quick detour through Jenel's Gems, looking at different pieces. Because he wanted to get Madeline something for Christmas. Something personal and meaningful.

When he left the jewelry store—still without the right present—he made sure Raven's jacket was snug and protecting her from the cold. The dog waited patiently while he did his check, then gave his hand a quick lick. He rubbed her ears.

"Let's go see Madeline," he told the dog.

They walked to Paper Moon and went inside. Madeline was finishing up with a bride. The other woman was wiping away tears.

"It's perfect," she said. "I love everything about it. Thank you for being so patient."

"I was happy to help. You're going to be a beautiful bride."

Two dresses on the same day, he thought. She would be happy about that. Because, as he'd thought before, they both made magic with their work. Only hers lasted a lifetime. Hers was filled with memories that were treasured.

She'd been sweet with his sister. Ginger hadn't stopped talking about how Madeline had handled everything. He appreciated that when the dress he'd ordered had arrived, she hadn't simply called him an idiot. She'd gone to the trouble of pressing it and putting his sister in it so he could *see* he was an idiot.

She was sweet and funny and easy to be with. She got his sense of humor and made him laugh in return. They were good together. They belonged together.

The last thought surprised him. He turned it over in his mind a few times and realized the truth had been staring at him all along.

Madeline was the one. He cared about her. No, he loved her.

Instinctively, he took a step back. No way. He couldn't. Loving her meant… Okay, he didn't know what it meant, but it was bad. Because loving someone was dangerous. He could lose her. An argument that usually worked for him, but not now. Not with Madeline. For the first time, the risk was worth the reward. He loved her.

He waited impatiently for the client to leave. When she did, he walked over to Madeline, prepared to tell her the good news.

Before he could figure out how to confess his feelings, she spoke first.

"I can't do this. I can't be with you. It's never going to work and you're not what I want. I've already talked to Dellina and she'll finish up the details for the wedding. I gave her your phone number. I'm sorry to be so abrupt, but I thought it best to tell you now. I hope..." She turned away, then looked back at him. "Goodbye."

He couldn't believe it. He had to not be hearing her right. None of this made sense. He was still trying to make sense of it all when he realized she was pushing him out the front door of her store and locking it behind him.

Just like that.

He didn't know why. Had she realized he wasn't a good bet? Had he convinced her being with him was going to be too hard? Or was it simply that life had a sense of humor—he'd finally managed to fall in love with someone, only to have her reject him two days before Christmas.

❧ SIXTEEN ❧

TWO HOURS LATER JONNY REALIZED how hard it would be without Madeline. He missed her. His house was empty and cold. Sure the temperature was fine—he didn't want Raven shivering—but still, it felt cold.

He wandered from room to room, not sure what to do with himself. He didn't know what had happened. Had she guessed he wasn't worth the trouble? Was she afraid? She'd never bought into the hype of him being a star. Did she see the man behind the mask and think there wasn't enough there? Or was it simply that she didn't care about him? That their time together had been fun, but nothing more?

He hadn't said anything to Ginger. He knew his sister was looking forward to having Madeline as part of her wedding. Somehow he would figure out an explanation—maybe when he understood what had happened.

Had he lost her because of who he was or because of who he wasn't?

He settled on the sofa in the family room and stared at the tree they'd decorated together. What had gone so very wrong and how did he now fix it? Because being without Madeline wasn't an option. The only question was how he convinced her to come back when he didn't know why he'd lost her in the first place.

Right up until eight-fifteen in the evening, Madeline knew she'd made the right decision. Loving Jonny was just crazy talk. There were a thousand reasons they couldn't make it work. Like how he... Well, there was...

He traveled, she thought at last. He was gone for weeks at a time. That would be hard. And he was famous. Everyone knew that famous people couldn't commit.

"Talk about ridiculous," she muttered. There had to be a better reason as to why she'd broken things off with him. Because if it wasn't him, it was her.

But that didn't make sense. She wanted to be in a relationship. She wanted to be in love. All her life she'd...

Messed up, she thought frantically. She'd failed. Made the wrong choice and had to backtrack to find her way again. She'd gone through multiple tries at finding the right career path. She'd had a string of failed relationships. While she'd finally found her dream job, she hadn't found her dream man.

Only Jonny was perfect. Okay, not perfect, but right for her. He was everything she'd been looking for and more and she'd…she'd…

Completely and totally freaked out. She'd panicked. She'd realized she loved him, had assumed he couldn't possibly love her back and had ended things before he could break her heart. Because what else was going to happen to an ordinary girl from Fool's Gold?

She hadn't given him a chance. Hadn't been brave enough to share her feelings. Tell him she loved him. Maybe he *was* going to say, "Thanks but no thanks," but maybe he wasn't. And even if he was, didn't she owe it to herself to hear it rather than just assume? Didn't being a grown-up mean doing the mature thing?

Better late than never, she thought, then wondered what she was supposed to do now. She'd dumped him without telling him why. Without admitting her feelings. Not behavior to be proud of. So how did she fix that?

She stood up and looked around her small place, as if the answer was there. She grabbed her phone, then realized a phone call or text wouldn't do. She had to face the man. Tell him the truth and then see what happened.

She got in her car and drove out to the ranch. Snow

fell and she had trouble seeing where she was going, but she didn't stop. She couldn't. She'd already given up too many times. She'd reacted out of fear, and she wasn't going to let that happen again.

She turned on the highway and kept her speed low. She fishtailed once, but steered into the skid, like her dad had taught her, and kept going. Her hands hurt from gripping the steering wheel, and despite the heater blasting hot air, she shivered in the cold.

What should have been a twenty-five-minute trip took over an hour, and when she finally pulled up in front of Jonny's house, she was shaken and exhausted. Tears burned. Fear grew until she had trouble breathing. What if he didn't love her? What if he couldn't forgive her? What if—

Her car door opened from the outside. She stared up at Jonny.

"Madeline? What's going on? I heard a car drive up. It's practically a blizzard. You shouldn't be driving. Are you okay?"

She flung herself at him. As she was wearing a seat belt, that didn't go well. She had to unfasten it and fling herself a second time. She wrapped her arms around him and hung on.

"I'm sorry," she told him. "I'm so sorry. I was wrong.

No, I was scared and wrong. I didn't give you a chance. I never told you the truth. I love you and that terrifies me. What if you don't love me back? What if you start dating Julia Roberts? Or Jennifer Lawrence? Or some other perfect star? What if—"

He pressed his fingers to her mouth to quiet her. "Shh," he murmured. "Let's get you inside."

She pushed his fingers away. "No. You have to understand. I love you. I want to be with you. I was so afraid. I lashed out and ran. Technically I pushed you away, but you know what I mean. I'm sorry."

He stared into her eyes for a long time. "I was scared, too," he admitted. "Scared of losing again. So I hid behind what I did because it was easier than admitting the truth. Even when Ginger tried to tell me, I wouldn't listen."

He smiled at her. "I love you, Madeline. I've been hiding from that for a while now, but I'm not going to anymore. I hadn't figured out how to convince you to give us a chance, but I was working on it."

"Really? You're not going to marry Julia Roberts?"

"She's already married and maybe a little old for me."

"Oh, right. So Jennifer Lawrence?"

"I'm going to marry you, if you'll have me."

"What?"

Was it her or had the snow suddenly started spinning? Okay, it was just her.

He drew her to the side, then got in her car and turned off the engine. After collecting her keys and her bag, he got out and then put his arm around her.

"Let's get into the house," he said. "You're shivering and I'm sure Raven is worried."

"You proposed." How could he be worried about something as mundane as cold when he'd just proposed?

"I did and I'd like an answer. But you're here and you love me, so the rest of it can wait."

They walked into the house. Raven greeted them both and then returned to her plaid bed. Jonny put Madeline's keys and bag on the entry table, before pulling her close and kissing her.

"Thank you for coming to see me," he said. "I was going to talk to you in the morning. I had no idea what I was going to say."

"You could have said I was an idiot."

"Probably not how I would have started."

She smiled up at him, then wrapped her arms around him. "I love you and I'm not letting go."

"Me, either. I love you, Madeline."

"Even though I'm ordinary?"

"Because you're extraordinary."

Words designed to make a girl weak at the knees. Who was she to try to be different?

She kissed him. "Yes, Jonny Blaze, I'll marry you." She grinned. "You know, there's a really beautiful dress just sitting in my office. Maybe I should try it on."

"Not your style."

"You sure about that?"

"Yes. But whatever you choose, you'll be beautiful and I'll be the luckiest man in the world."

He put his arm around her and led her into the family room. They settled on the sofa, near the tree, and hung on to each other. She rested her head on his shoulder.

"Let's not tell anyone until after Ginger's wedding," she said. "About us. The day should be about her and Oliver. I don't want to distract from that."

Instead of answering, Jonny kissed her. He wrapped his arms around her and lowered her back on the sofa. As his body moved over hers, she knew that the sparks she felt were so much more. They were bolts of lightning... just like she'd been promised.

EPILOGUE

JONNY SMILED AT HIS SISTER. "You're beautiful."

"Thanks. I'm nervous. I didn't think I would be, but I am."

They stood in the alcove of the converted barn. All the guests were in place and music played. Oliver stood with his brother and Mayor Marsha, who would be marrying the couple. The woman had many skills, he thought.

"You're sure about this guy?" he asked.

Ginger relaxed. "I am. He's the one. I love him." She hugged Jonny. "Thank you for my beautiful wedding. It's perfect."

He glanced at the twinkle lights and the flowers, the way the chairs were set up, the long center aisle, covered in rose petals. At the other end of the barn, the tables were ready. Candles glowed and the dishes were in place.

He knew that Madeline had already confirmed everything. That Ana Raquel and her husband were prepared with the food and the bar stations were stocked. Out-side, ice sculptures gleamed in the clear night. Flood-lights marked the path to the house.

"I'm glad you're happy," he told his sister. "I had a good time planning your wedding."

She laughed softly. "You did an excellent job. It's much less over the top than I expected. No fireworks."

He thought about the show scheduled to start at nine. "You might want to wait on that one."

Her eyes widened. "Seriously?"

"It'll only last about five minutes."

Ginger hugged him. "Honestly, I don't know if I should laugh or slug you."

"I vote for laughing." He touched her chin, raising her head so their eyes met. "I love you, Ginger. I want you to be happy."

"I am, and I love you, too." She pressed her lips to-gether. "This is a change. I didn't think I would ever hear you say those words again." Her expression brightened. "Oh, wow. Is it because of Madeline? I thought I felt a connection between the two of you."

"Good guess."

Ginger hugged him again. "I'm so happy for you. She's great. I like her a lot."

The music shifted to the wedding march and the guests all rose.

"That's our cue," Jonny told her. "You ready?"

"I am."

She tucked her arm in his and they started down the aisle. He nodded at the people he knew, then found the one person who mattered most.

Madeline stood next to the seat she was saving for him. Tears filled her eyes, but he knew they were the happy ones. The good ones. He'd seen similar tears when he'd given her the engagement ring he'd picked out. The ring that was tucked in her nightstand drawer for the evening.

Later, when the happy couple was back from their honeymoon, the four of them would have dinner and he and Madeline would announcement their engagement.

They were already making wedding plans. Nothing too big, Madeline had told him. Or over the top. As he kissed Ginger's cheek and watched as Oliver drew her close, he wondered if he really could fly in the Vienna Boys' Choir. Just for a couple of songs.

★ ★ ★ ★ ★